Item
as

DAD'S RED DRESS

L. J. Sedgwick

First Edition | 2017

Janey Mac Books

Cover Design by Aoife Henkes
Formatting by Polgarus Studio

Print Version
ISBN-13: 978-0995702707
ISBN-10: 0995702705

Published by Janey Mac Books

ONE

If it wasn't my entire life being loaded into the removal truck, it would be fun to watch. "No! Careful! Salome is delicate, yes?" Eva, my step-mum, is supervising the removal men. "You need to lift her this way so the eyes are not upside down and her ears don't crack like lice."

Ice. She means 'ice'.

They stop work until Dad opens the crate to show them Salome is a statue, not a dead body. Eva's an artist. '*Half-woman, half-wolf*', that's how she wanted to describe herself on the last census but Dad said, "Best not". Right now, she's in a dress she made from scarves, every colour and hue. On her, well she looks like a rainbow cos she is really tall and thin like spaghetti. Despite eating more than any of us, which seems deeply unfair. Today, there's even a silky purple scarf hanging down her back like a tail. It was meant to be keeping her hair back but escaped and got caught on the catch of her necklace.

Laura watches everything from a handstand. My sister is lanky and seven, insists on wearing a little white veil and

1

honestly, having Salome for a sister would be easier. Unlike Laura, Salome doesn't think she was abducted by the Virgin Mary.

Twice.

Once on a motorbike, with a pink afro.

Today is the day I've been dreading for weeks. We're leaving L.A. Heading 'home' to Ireland. Even though I was five when we last visited and despite the fact that Laura and I were both born here, while Eva is Chilean. Dad says America was an experiment, similar to growing an ear on a mouse or inventing a bra that comes apart into two gas masks in case of chemical attack. *'You can save the man of your choice'*, says the ad.

Fat chance.

Unless I magically acquire boy-magnet status in Dublin.

As for the timing of the move, Eva says it's now or never cos Dad is turning American and it's only a matter of time before he starts walking with a drawl in his legs and maybe wearing caps backwards and understanding baseball. Nobody mentions Bethany or what she saw or said she saw to exactly EVERYONE in the school yard. Which wasn't even as bad as saying I'd grown a tail from my nose, that my father was a poet or that my kid sister kept a foul-smelling scruffiluffigous monster in the back yard.

Although, if she had kept one, I would definitely have asked it to gobble up my so-called school FRIENDS, but especially Bethany. (Face first, dipped in tomato sauce; screams recorded on my iPhone for instant YouTube upload to the tune of *Dancing Queen* cos it's awful. Like her.)

Most of the crates are packed now, including one with the model Dad and I made of this house in the last few weeks. We've done these when we moved before. Dad's an architect but this one I'm going to finish myself. I've stolen little bits of carpet so it can really be identical and taken dozens of photos. It's a way of accepting the move, says Dad, but this time I'm not sure. In case his theory doesn't work, I've stuffed all the empty rooms with Tootsie Rolls, Sour Patches and Reeses to help with the homesickness I fully expect to hit.

See, while Dad says we're moving 'home' or 'back', all I remember is here.

I leave them to it and roam the house one more time. It doesn't feel like ours now, empty of everything, so I wander out back and lie on the lawn, staring at the most magnificent clouds. I still can't believe we're really leaving America. Hot dogs and sunshine and ice dispensers in ginormous fridges you could hide a polar bear inside and not even notice footprints in the butter…

Maybe if I stay here, really quietly, they'll forget to take me.

~ ~ ~

"Passengers Frank, Laura and Jessica Keane and Eva Moreno, travelling to Dublin, your flight is fully boarded and closing at Gate…"

We board the plane untidily, deluged by dirty looks as the passengers realise they were delayed for us. Laura bags the window seat in case she spots God in passing but we all know Santa would do. Settling her veil, she tells God that while *she's* ready to plunge to her death in a burning plane, we're not so maybe he could wait?

And if he wants to drop by, could he tap the window gently so he doesn't make her jump. Then she falls asleep.

Why can't she play Nintendo like everybody else?

Dad says we have to pretend the veil is not there. She has been wearing it for a year but people still stare and go, "Oh Sweetheart! That cute little girl! Did you just do your Holy Communion, child?"

I reach over to tug it off but she has it attached with an army of pins any one of which could be a high calibre assassination weapon for a medium-sized ogre. She doesn't even stir.

Dad leans in. "The weather in Ireland will do it for the veil. You can't wear a veil under a raincoat."

I bet Laura can.

He takes Eva's hand and smiles at her, as if he's the luckiest, happiest man alive. If they kiss the plane will fall out of the sky from embarrassment.

When Dad was Laura's age, he wanted to be a cat after his parents took him to see the musical *Cats*. Wouldn't talk for weeks except in miaows and he stuck whiskers to his cheeks with super glue. Maybe this is why he can be so understanding about Laura's veil.

As we take off, Dad slips off his sneakers and puts on gold pumps. They're his lucky pumps. He's a bit superstitious about flying. I fix the blanket over his lap. "Your feet'll get cold."

"You're too good."

Eva's already asleep. All she has to do is imagine standing under a warm waterfall or that she's a kitten in a paddock full of furry dust-balls and she's gone. Trouble is, she also *hums* in her sleep which is weird but not *wonderful* weird as she ALWAYS hums out of tune.

I mean, *REALLY* out of tune.

At first, I used to joke she was emitting audio landing signals for some spaceship full of gremlins. Then I got to like her. She makes Dad happy and I didn't think that was possible after, well, Mum n all. Laura, she's mad about her. Like a rabbit caught in a blaze of light.

You can't fight that.

At least Bethany has absolutely NO Irish rellies. Not even a distant singular watered-down Irish gene so I won't meet her 19th cousin, even accidentally.

We are flying in on the tail-end of winter, tripping into Dublin on the rolled-up carpet-edge of spring to start our new life.

Eva says it's "auspicious".

I hope that's a good thing.

TWO

Dublin. Suburbia. All neat hedges and twitching curtains. Our house is near the curved bottom of a cul de sac on Dublin's northside, facing a green patch of prickly bushes and a big black bin. We're not far from the sea, says Dad. There's a regular bus service to town, shops and even a cafe ten minutes walk away but it still feels like the end of the world.

And cold. It definitely feels cold!

All our worldly goods and Eva's statues are scattered in front of a house that Dad is the only one to have seen before now. Her statues are life-size and nude, which means life-sized naked and dangly bits. They will be the central pieces of her first Irish exhibition in a month's time but I'm not sure the twitchers appreciate their artistic value.

My all time favourite is *Ulysses*; hair carved into a ship with a handbag full of miniature but very beautiful sheep on his lap. He was the first she made when she was with us so nobody really wants him to sell, not even Eva.

Laura's tank is upended onto the driveway by the movers.

6

They've barely put it down when this little dog wees up against it and Laura chases him off making menacing noises. Didn't I mention the tank? It's for Ponchinello, her piranha. He has travelled with us surreptitiously. Don't ask how. Suffice it to say, her veil is nothing to the wailing she made when told her beloved fish couldn't come with us but at least here there isn't room for the tank in our bedroom here since it stinks. Laura refuses to clean off the algae as it's a living organism and "might have a soul".

One day, I swear I'll shred that veil and feed her to lions.

I'm sure it's wrong to feed kid sisters to lions. Even if they are hungry.

The house is not EXACTLY what I'd expected. Compared to our house in L.A., it's small; a post-war semi-d with ivy sneaking up the wall. There's a large dormer window in the roof which means we can probably use the attic and a gi-normous oak fills the front lawn. At least, I presume it's an oak since *The Oaks* is the name of the estate.

But get this, while all the other houses are pretty identical except for porches and extensions, the house flanking ours – the other semi-to our house – is *wild*.

Seriously.

For starts, the front door has a Roman pagoda built around it, with pillars and a tympanum full of constipated cherubs. Where their path borders the pavement, they have erected this enormous wooden archway. It's probably meant to be covered by the trailing jasmine that's about six inches high on each side but there isn't even a wall on either side, just a piddly little fence a mouse could hop over.

"Whatcha think?"

I drag my eyes away from the cherubs. Dad has draped himself around Eva's most recent nude. This half man, half woman, with wings and pointed ears, is called *Passion/ Fruit*. Right now, Dad's knee lolls over one of its hands, his arm is round its waist and he's grinning as if this is a photo shoot for Hello. Forget that his hair is standing on end from the static of the last flight and could be used in a model of gone-wrong spaghetti for vegetarian ogres with poor eyesight or that all our new neighbours are probably taking notes, it's still not a good look.

"Too young?"

"Yup, Dad. That's the ONLY problem!"

"You're right."

Eva leaves the house to supervise Angel's journey to her studio in the back garden. "Tell me you love me, Eva Moreno," he says, "before my heart crumbles to dust."

"No." She grins, trying to peel him off so the movers can, well, move the statue down to her studio in the back yard. "You are smelly and messy from the flight and you prefer Passion/Fruit to me!"

"What was that, Light of my Life?" He grabs her in an embrace. They always look odd together, she's so much taller than him but neither of them care.

"Okay," says Eva, taking her time. "Since you asked nicely, I love you." And they kiss. And kiss and kiss... GOD! Parents can be SO embarrassing. I've told them if they ONCE use tongues in front of me, I'm putting myself up for adoption.

~ ~ ~

"He's an Amazonian piranha. They're very highly strung."
Laura has cornered the movers as they heft her tank inside.
"He might not even eat Irish flies. In which case, I'm going
to see if he'll take to beetles, cos they'd be meatier."

I think it's an underdog thing. Find the ugliest, nastiest,
most reptilian fish, give it the personality of a snare gun and
that's Ponchinello. He doesn't make friends since he tends
to eat anything that falls into his water before they can strike
up any sort of terrified conversation.

At least Dad has convinced her to stop hanging pumice
stones into the tank – she wanted him to be able to sharpen
his teeth – while I feed him lollipops when she's not looking
so he's probably nearly harmless now.

I wouldn't recommend you try, all the same, to shake
hands.

~ ~ ~

It's so old fashioned inside. Proper polished banisters. A
carpet with tiny flowers that look poisonous. There's even a
lamp in the hallway with stained glass roses that match those
in the hall door window. Dad only saw the house twice. Any
work that needed doing, he had to tell builders what to do
from L.A. so the decor, he said, would have to wait until
we'd settled in.

He had the room I'm sharing with Laura painted yellow
to brighten it up. Apparently it was green before and we both
hate green. Ironic, since it's the colour of our new school

uniform. The big oak is right outside, its branches long enough to touch the window. I bet they give us mini heart attacks during every windy night for the next year.

"Forget that. Come see this," says Dad, leading me past crates and boxes and bags waiting to be unpacked, up twisty little stairs at the end of the landing and into the attic. He's like a skinny puppy on razorblades but I was right about the attic! It's enormous, full of desks and bright because there are these big windows on both sides. Only some of them are not windows, they're doors; I know because he's flinging them open.

I step past him onto this most amazing balcony that runs the length of the back of the house. At the end of the garden, Eva's working out where everything should go in her studio. But 'up' is better. *'Up'* is sky and clouds and nothing else.

"Cool," says Laura, sticking her head out and then she's gone.

Dad stays inside. He has to, since he can NOT manage heights. Even little ones. Laura would scale a ladder to the moon and stop half way to admire the view. Me, I'd make the first three steps but Dad wouldn't put his toes on the first rung.

He says *he* has vertigo while *I'm* just a scaredy cat.

"Your own personal Cloud Platform," says Dad. "Thought you'd appreciate having your own space to chill in."

"I love it."

Dad and I have this thing about clouds. See, clouds can lift you up out of whatever is bothering you and when you're finished, it doesn't bother you so much anymore. Before we left L.A., when I was lying out back, I watched a cloud crocodile gobble Bethany. It made me feel calmer to be leaving. She was probably snogging Carlo instead, right at that moment. Carlo who was *meant* to fancy me, but I told myself that it didn't matter cos I hadn't quite got over the *boys-are-noisy-and-they-stink* phase yet.

"Well?" says Dad. "Anything?"

I squint and scan the sky but I can't identify a single identifiable shape. All I can see is Laura dancing with Eva in the studio. She's totally at home; with her eyes closed, she wouldn't knock into anything. I'm all thumbs and elbows unless it's a scale model of a building and I have a glue gun in my hand, so I don't go into her studio much.

Definitely not this close to a show.

"Nothing?"

Maybe clouds are easier to 'read' in L.A.; they KNOW they have to impress. You look up casually, maybe walking to school, wondering how to explain that you never did your Math homework, and there's a bank robber in the sky. She's wearing an elephant mask and dragging a getaway car from the cloud behind. So you know not to go to the bank today and to steer REAL clear of elephants.

Or there's a three-headed silver man being hauled through the sky by a beautiful but arrogant Princess, which means *'don't bother ringing Bethany today, she'll only stand you up'*.

Suddenly I'm homesick for our old house, all our homes, for the way we were when Mum… I turn my back on the view and head inside. "I need to unpack."

"Come here Squirrel." In the safety of the attic, Dad wraps his arms around me. "Long day, huh?" I'm nodding and feel I might cry, which is something I don't want to do in case i can't stop, when I'm saved by this tooting of horns. Laura shouts up the stairs as she tears through the house, "They're here! Gramma and Gaffa are HERE!"

See, that's what I love about my irritating kid sister. She wears her heart on her sleeve. And when it comes to Gramma and Gaffa, it's a very big heart. After all, they're the real reason we're here.

Family.

~~~

By the time we come out, Laura is hopping from foot to foot with this idiotic grin on her face. "Meet the panther," says Gaffa to Dad, patting his black car on the rump and swinging open the passenger door to free Gramma.

"So what?" she says, hugging Laura and me but eyeing Dad, "You were just going to sneak in?"

Gramma gives the best hugs. They're warm and soft and grippy all at once. Sometimes I want to stay there and never come out. Laura used to hug me like that. I mean, when she was little and I lifted her into bed and her fingers curled around my neck.

"There, there," she says and lets me hold on a little more.

"Great to see you, Gramma," I manage, between sniffs. It's only tiredness from the flight. I'm NOT a crier. Ask anyone.

"So how are my favourite grandkids?" She pulls back to examine each of us in turn and acts as if the veil isn't there, which is Dad's doing.

"Your *only* grandkids," says Laura, grinning.

"Told her you'd like time to settle in first but there was no stopping her," says Gaffa. "She'd have been on the flight home with you if she could."

Which is daft.

We lived in America. Why would she fly to America just to fly home with us?

Gramma hands out housewarming gifts. Laura gets goldfish because Gramma doesn't know she smuggled Ponchinello over and thinks Laura might need fish-consoling. Eva gets Chilean wine because she believes Eva has made the biggest sacrifice, moving here for us.

Me, I get the most perfect little orange kitten called Buffy.

"A friend to help you settle in, Jessica," she says; *Gramma*, not the cat. That would be weird. But nice weird. We could discuss how to kill Ponchinello together and she could spy for me and I'd have a new best friend that could never let me down… She always tries to call me Jessica cos she says a 'right Jessie' was what people say here when you're dim and I'm not.

"Ponchinello's swimming upside down. Dad says it's cos he thinks we're still in L.A."

"Oh, you brought your fish…"

Laura drags Gramma inside. "And he's black, but he turned black before we left."

"Probably because he ate the other goldfish Dad got

you," I hiss but she ignores me. She's determined to find Ponchinello a friend that will cross the fish species divide. All that has happened so far is that Ponchinello has been able to hunt his own food – five goldfish, one clown fish, several cat fish and the rest.

"I'm sure he's fine," says Gramma. She doesn't like him either.

"So." Gaffa punches Dad in the upper arm. "You missed the match."

After a quick tour of the house, Gramma unpacks this full meat n veg n trimmings dinner for us. As a meal, being homemade, it is divine and, for us, highly unusual. Eva does wicked salads; Dad does frozen or takeaway and anything that involves sausages.

During dessert, Buffy tries to get into Ponchinello's tank. Dad starts sneezing when he lifts her off and hands her to me.

"Oh, Silly me! That's right," says Gramma. "You used to be allergic to cats. It was right after you stuck whiskers on your cheeks. I completely forgot."

So when Buffy decides to have a lengthy wee on Ulysses – our temporary coat hanger cos there isn't room for him in her studio yet –, and Dad sneezes so much that he can't eat pudding, Buffy gets exiled to our room. This is when I get rewarded for NOT slagging Laura off about her veil: Buffy, officially my new best friend in the world because she clearly understands that Laura is a PAIN, wees on Laura's bed.

Unfortunately, she misses Laura's bag of spare veils, but you can't have everything.

THREE

I colonise our room – sorry, *my* room in which I allow Laura to sleep – on the principle of *'first come, best served, dragons eat the princesses all the time and never complain of tummy ache'*. Right now, mid-afternoon, it's far too bright. It's like staring into a pet vampire's eyes when they've turned to gold. More werewolf than night owl, I choose the darkest half and stow my model house full of Reeses, Tootsie Rolls and Sour Patches under the bed. I'm tempted to dip into them but they're too precious for casual snacking. I have to reserve my supplies.

The door bell rings as I unpack my books. Naturally, I ignore it. Probably someone wanting us to join a cult where everyone sits cross-legged and bounces up and down shouting *pizza!*

"Jessie!"

Actually, that doesn't sound so bad. Provided a few of the cult members are stunning guys like Carlo. I'm not saying I fancied him. But I could have, if he'd fancied me madly. I mean, I'd have made an effort!

"Jessie, will you answer the door!"

"Why me?"

"Send Laura if you want to practice being a grumpy teenager."

"I am grumpy teenager and she's bagging bugs."

"Already?" Dad's in his favourite pale blue dress with a wraparound cardi. Okay, so he can't answer the door.

"Says they're sleepier in the afternoon and easier to catch."

The bell rings AGAIN.

"Don't expect me to be nice!" I stomp downstairs and fling the door open. Facing me is one of those women you don't know whether to invite in or tie to the gatepost and feed entrails as you wait for her to transform back into a demon.

How can ANYONE put that much time and effort into appearing *dull*?

However, I am also face to face with the most GORGEOUS cake in the world and Dad says we should always try to see the best in everyone, to look past the things we don't like that they might not even have meant to do or say. Except bigots, who hate people for no reason and violent criminals.

She says she's from next door and her name is "*Jennifer, with a J*", which I think must be some sort of joke I don't get. I show her into the living room where Laura's lecturing Ponchinello about self esteem and treating other fish with respect. Her new goldfish are in a Pyrex bowl flanked by the tank and Buffy.

Honestly, if I were them, I'd prefer my chances with the cat.

"Why didn't you answer the door?"

"Mum said not to."

I let it go. It's not as if she ever really knew Mum, which seems unfair enough without challenging her imaginary conversations with her too. Besides, we have a visitor. Laura's good with visitors.

Mostly.

"I was abducted by the Virgin Mary twice when we lived in L.A. but it hasn't happened for a long time. I think she must be pretty busy."

"Oh," says Jennifer.

Okay, she's *normally* good. Normally she doesn't talk about her abductions until visitors are a good ten minutes in and the cake has been handed over intact.

"Not now, Laura," I say in a tone that says to Jennifer, *'My sister, she does get odd ideas but it's okay. It's not real. We are really normal'.* Jennifer smiles straight back and looks around. She's our own, personal nosy neighbour. "Dad'll be right down."

"Would you like to meet Ponchinello? I can fish him out and you could stroke him?"

"That's not a good idea, Laura."

"Better to leave him in the water, I think. But I'd love to take a look." She's being polite. Adults shouldn't do this around Laura; it only encourages her. "Do you know, Laura, we used to keep fish when I was a child. My father was a dentist. We had this large tank in the waiting room."

Laura selects the plumpest bug from a handful in her pocket. I should really stop her, but this could be fun. "Eva said I should make sure he isn't hungry before I introduce him to his new friends," she says and drops the bug into the tank.

For a beat, nothing happens.

Then, very suddenly, Ponchinello tears his eyes away from the goldfish in the Bowl Next Door and opens a mouth bigger than his entire body, full of small, very sharp teeth. Chomp. The bug is gone. I can't imagine he'd recovered from the shock of being in Laura's pocket let alone the water so he probably wasn't even scared of the fish.

I wonder if bugs have religion?

Jennifer freezes. "Oh!" she pops. "Is that–?" And steps back so smartly that she falls into the couch. Laura's goldfish flee to the farthest side of their bowl and swim in a vertical line, like a sort of golden ladder of impossible escape. This could be how evolution began. All that was really needed were a few carnivorous fish for amoeba to discover they could morph legs and wings after all.

When Jennifer pulls herself free, she pops all over again.

"You whiffed," says Laura, grinning.

"I did not. That was your sofa."

"Yes, you did. I can smell it."

"It *was* the sofa, Laura," I say as Dad and Eva enter, all smiles.

Eva has a boob in her hand but in the circumstances, I don't think our guest notices. It's a plaster cast for pieces that will make up one of her installations. Dad's nicknamed it her *Field of Mammaries* but she probably has some long mythical female-empowering title for it.

Jennifer holds out her cake to Eva. "Hard to find time to bake when you've just moved."

Eva hands me her boob and the women shake hands.

Sensing she's losing her audience, Laura drops a goldfish into the tank. It's not exactly a meeting of minds. Ponchinello simply opens his mouth – you can almost hear the yawn – and swallows.

Bye bye, Goldfish Number One.

Laura catches us staring and shrugs. "I just have to feed him more."

Our visitor doesn't stay long after that. She leaves us an information sheet about all the local committees, the community association, the book club, Tidy Town and Clean Up Day. "Great to have fresh blood in the estate," she says to Eva, which is appropriate when you're in a room with Ponchinello.

Deciding that we're unlikely to have any more visitors, Dad slips back into his dress and we order takeaway pizza.

Dad only dresses like this because that's how he feels inside; he *feels* that he should have been a girl, which is pretty messed up for him. Since Eva started helping him shop though, he wears dresses and skirts that actually suit him and it's no big deal. It makes him feel good inside.

Same way pizza does for me.

~ ~ ~

It's not even nine o'clock when Dad produces this box of costumes he found in the attic when the previous owners left. If one of the perks of being the Big Sister is a later bedtime, one of the disadvantages of having a dad who cross-dresses is that he's liable to want to try on any costume and Eva is far too understanding.

How do you think Laura saw the Virgin Mary on a motorbike with a pink afro? It was Dad returning from a New Year's Eve fancy dress party. They're really good gigs for him. He usually aims for a female super hero but he does NOT make a good Wonder Woman!

So this time, I am GONE!

Besides, I know, for a fact, that as soon as my head hits the pillow – gently, cos it's a very tired head, – I will sleep like a vampire at spring-time in Antarctica.

~ ~ ~

But I don't.

Don't with a capital *D.O.N.*APOSTROPHE *T.*

It happens from time to time and it's never fun.

I have tried counting sheep only MY sheep go on strike, slip in sheep poo or crash headlong into the gate. Deliberately. The theatrical ones balance on the gate reciting *To Be Or Not To Be* or doing cartwheels while giving out about something.

The worst is when they start telling jokes cos they are usually really, REALLY bad. Sheep, especially imaginary ones, are useless at telling jokes.

Tonight I try counting tiny Laura's being chased by a werewolf through a forest but it's too much fun. I don't have the patience to stay in bed when I can't sleep so I get up and take the model of the old house out from under the bed and hide all the sweets in a box so I can look at it properly. It's pretty neat really. All the dimensions are exactly to measure, but since I can't fit in and go back in time, it doesn't help me, not now.

Laura's still twitching in her little veil when I get bored and slip downstairs. Eva and Dad are dancing on the patio, lit by the studio. It's kind of sweet. I mean, when parents aren't being annoying and embarrassing, it's nice to see them happy.

I put Buffy on the counter with a snatch of chicken skin left from Gramma's dinner while I pour a glass of water. Which is when I spot this guy up a tree next door.

Who prunes trees at night?!

Clearly the sight of two people dancing in dresses is distracting cos next thing you know, he cuts through the branch his ladder is leaning against and SNAP! Buffy leaps into my arms and the man vanishes down into his own back yard. Dad and Eva carry on waltzing. They have no idea they have been gawked at by this man.

Must suggest quick-growing firs to replace the hedge.

Sometimes I reckon the universe wants me to find something out and stops me sleeping until I have, because Laura sleeps like an unused blog every night bar none. See now, right when Buffy's purring is making my tummy vibrate and I've decided to go back to bed, thinking *now* I'll sleep, Eva stops dancing and lays Dad's hand on her tummy.

He looks down at his hand and then up into her eyes for the longest moment and she nods. He whoops like a baby rhino so she has to shush him, but she's laughing all the time and he hugs her instead. Hugs and hugs and hugs…

And I know we're going to have a baby.

FOUR

Friday.

First day of the rest of our lives.

"No time to brood" in Eva-speak equals "making tons of friends".

That's how it's supposed to happen.

Beyond the school gates is a wasteland of tarmac, teeming with boys – smelly, noisy, *push you out of the way just to get a snigger* sort of boys – and girls with attitude.

St Brigid's is one of those schools that "nurtures the individual". Which is obviously why the uniform closely resembles prison issue and the girls are forced to wear skirts regardless of the weather. Right. The *individual. Nurtured.* I take Laura's hand. She's my human shield. Dad made us memories a map of the two schools – elementary to the left, secondary right ahead – when we wouldn't let him come with us. I almost regret that now but we're not kids and we can't be seen to be brought to school by a parent, not if we are to have any chance of fitting in. One more deep breath and we walk through the gate, overweight rucks hanging off

22

our shoulders like well-fed cows.

Laura scans the yard to see if she can spot a real nun but the best she can find is a Muslim girl in a hajib. Ahead of us, a circle of Neanderthals have gathered around a small boy in glasses. He has to be smaller. Bullies are useless unless their victims are smaller.

The leader of this intelligent posse is a red-haired genius, one of those boys who shoots up tall before he learns to join words into sentences.

The victim probably has brains cos that'd REALLY annoy the tall-but-clearly-dim thug. And it's all about a bag. A *school* bag! Like, boys! Seriously? We know you're not as mature as us but why would anyone bother stealing a SCHOOL bag? While I ponder this, Laura steps into the circle and stands beside the boy.

As a human shield, since I'm still holding her hand, she has her drawbacks.

While I'm pondering this, Laura whips her veil from her bag and puts it on. Before the gang snaps out of its collective Wicker Man-Shaun of the Dead zombie trance, I grab the bag and hand it to the bullied boy who nods and runs off.

Laura and I move on through, not a single word spoken.

How cool is that? First day at school and we're flicking bullies off bikes. Actually, that's probably NOT a good thing to do on your first day. Nor is wearing a veil, but as I'm thinking this, there's a chorus of little half-hidden cheers all around. Some kids follow us and act as if Laura's magical.

Which she is, really. Or would be, if she wasn't my sister and I didn't know what she does to dolls. (Think 'trying out tortures a nun in medieval times might have had to face' and you're not even close.) I decide a veil's not bad. She could be into tattoos like Bethany.

Or she could be a boy.

Feeling all proud and big sisterly, I walk her right to the door of Room 16 in the elementary school – sorry, *junior* school. I even give her a hug, but only a little one cos she's in her veil and it's my first day too. "Meet you by the main gate after Homework Club." This has been arranged by Dad so we can walk home together.

"Sure," she says and trots right in.

Which leaves me to fight my way back through the swamp of littlies – they're worse than midges – chattering their way to class. By the time I trudge up to the old convent building, the yard is empty and there's a nun by the door looking like an Ogham stone.

"Five minutes more and you'd be late," she says, tapping her watch. Which, surely, means I'm on time?

Or I will be. If I can find classroom 2D.

~ ~ ~

I don't even have time to wonder why I'm in a class that sounds like a training bra, because 2D is nowhere near 2A or 2B. "2D?" says this boy when I pass him for the third time. I nod. "Out back. Third prefab on the left."

He has the brownest eyes. They look kind but maybe that's only because I want them to be cos he is SERIOUSLY cute. "Thanks," I manage.

I don't think I ever really fancied anyone before. Not

24

even celebrities, though I said I did. Today is NOT the day to start but he is GORGEOUS.

"But on Fridays, there's Assembly first thing, in the Hall," he says. "I'd show you but I have to get something from my locker," which is when I realise I'm glued to the spot like a spiky bonsai.

"Yeah, right. Thanks." I make my feet move.

"That way." He smiles, pointing the opposite direction.

"Are you in 2D?" Yup, it just popped out. He points to the room behind him. 3A. See, not stupid, me; I checked where he lives. Just in case. Well, you never know. New school, new rules, new fanciable me…

Another bell goes.

I have no idea how many bells have been rung now but I CAN'T be late on the first day so the great impression I leave with the boy is of me skidding down the far-too-highly polished corridor, round the corner and SPLAT! into a tall man in a suit.

And no, I do NOT land alongside or beside him on the ground. I land ON him. Completely. Nose to nose and the taste of aftershave – hideous, crushed bug slime n sweat – in my pores and the echo chambers of my ears.

Why could this not have happened anywhere else? As in America, with Carlos being the one I landed on?

As if that wasn't enough, his mug of coffee flies up into the air as we collide like the Big Bang, completes a neatly executed triple flip dive and spills its entire contents over this woman behind him. Two in one go.

It's not easy, getting up off a flattened teacher. There are elbows and knees and hands to manage without doing further damage to the body beneath you. The woman who gets the acrobatic black coffee is angular, her hair like a horse's whip. The coffee covers her jumper as if rediscovering its soul mate.

Okay, I think. *We all look the same in this snot-coloured uniform.* I apologise sincerely to both, avoid eye contact, hope my fringe is long enough to turn me into an unmemorable bison and vanish down the corridor into Assembly. If there is to be any hope for me in this school – and I call on every pagan god I can think of to support me in this – then the man I floored and the woman he drenched are parents who got mislaid, not teachers.

Or, at least, not *my* teachers.

~ ~ ~

Assembly is long and monotonous. Detentions are announced and rules and regulations reiterated, "As some people seem to have forgotten them". As I'm drifting off, the Principal adds, "We have a new addition to our school this week all the way from America."

Suddenly I am aware of every stitch that went into my shoes, studying them with deep concentration.

This can NOT be happening.

"Ms Jessica Keane?" I feel him comb the crowd. "Show us a hand, Jessica. Don't be shy." No WAY. "She should be in," he confers with another teacher, "2D? Can anyone find her?"

Of course, I'm in the wrong class group so I raise my

hand very slowly and only because the alternative is a 'where's Wally' hunt for me. The whole room has a good gawk and I get a clear view of the man who has publicly embarrassed me.

Pagan gods clearly have a twisted sense of humour.

See, last time we met, this Principal and me, he was flat on his back.

Great.

Roll on the next five years.

FIVE

2D is the third in a line of prefabs nuzzling the back wall of the school; small, orphaned shoe-boxes hoping to be brought inside. Thinking I'm the teacher, I get to bask in the glare of 29 pairs of eyes before the noise explodes again. It's like a swamp at feeding time and smells of sweaty feet. Two boys stand on top of their tables – wobbly, Formica – doing competitive press-ups against the wall. Why? They're boys, I guess.

I hate starting a new school mid-term. You've no idea what the rules are, who's buds with who and what the popular stuff is or the stuff that will pigeonhole you as a dork forever. As I weave towards a spare table half way down, I pick up stray words about a student falling for a teacher and I think, 'Ugh, who would want to do that!' Then I see Bully Boy perched on a desk in the farthest corner with the biggest, most evil grin and I realise that they're talking about ME.

Which is another YAHOO from me right there.

At least I've beaten our teacher to class so I won't start out with a bad mark.

Cue door CREAKING open; *Addams Family* meets *Gone With the Wind*. In comes this grumpy-looking, COFFEE-SPLATTERED woman who, it transpires, is Ms O'Flaherty, our form tutor, who teaches Religion and Spanish.

Brilliant.

"I see we have the new girl," she says, rolling her rs. "Why don't you come up front, Jessica and introduce yourself to the WHOLE class?" She adds something about not wanting to SPRING it on me, which makes the whole class snigger. The coffee stain on her jumper resembles a lumpy Gremlin with seven wobbly legs but I'm sure it's an improvement.

I'm also pretty sure she wouldn't agree.

What can I do? I tell them my name, that I have a little sister and that we've just moved over from L.A…. Blah blah Beelzebub blah.

"Oh don't stop," says Ms O'Flaherty, sweetly taking her revenge. She knows it. I know it. The rest of the class couldn't be more bored. Someone at the back is making fake fart noises and I'm guessing it's the Warthog. "I'm sure everyone would love to hear a LOT more detail. Favourite food, favourite colour, most embarrassing moment?"

Two can play this game. I go 'family' instead. "Dad's a Creative Architect. People take him on to design buildings that will challenge perceptions of light and space. He's usually inspired by ancient structures or sites, such as the pyramids or the Coliseum. The last big one was an Irish heritage centre outside L.A.

"He was headhunted back here, some hush-hush project I'm not allowed to talk about involving dead bodies." *That* at least gets the right attention. "Played rugby for Leinster too. Eva, my step-mum, she's an artist. She's got an exhibition coming up in a month–"

"What's L.A. like?"

"Hot."

"I'll bet!" The Bully Beast sniggers. He's thinking of topless models rather than the weather.

"What's it *actually* like to live there?" asks a girl with long, bored hair. It's so straight, she must sleep with it in a cardboard bag or get up three hours before the rest of us to tame it. "Did you meet any celebrities?"

"We sort of lived in the suburbs."

"What's the point of living in L.A. if you didn't get to meet any celebs!?" There's a snigger that the teacher stops with a look.

"Oh! You mean *actors*!?" There's a chorus of 'dohs' and 'obviously'.

"Oh, sure. Heaps." That shuts them up. Like alligators sensing tourists and sun cream, they can afford to wait. "Tom Cruise asked Dad to design a beach house." Okay, so it was the *firm* Dad worked for that Cruise's agent approached and the project fell through before Dad got involved but why tell them that? "Colin Farrell, he stayed next door for a while." Sorry, Colin was staying in a nearby suburb. Pagan gods, you haven't exactly been kind to me today so please don't smite me down! I'm only stretching the truth a little.

Once the fibs start, it's hard to hold back. "Penelope Cruz, she came to my tenth birthday party and Hannah Montana came to the last one."

"That's not her real name!"

"She came as Hannah, to sing for us. One Direction was meant to perform but Harry got a sore throat." Ms O'Flaherty decides this is going far too well for me and sets us an exercise memorising the names of the books in the Old Testament. Obviously, she wants to punish us for being teenagers.

~ ~ ~

Double PE before lunch. If I can make it out onto the field, the day might not end up with me needing to be exorcised. You can't be quizzed when you're a mad thing tearing round a patch of grass. Imagine my JOY when I've barely got my sports bag unzipped and I hear, "You didn't really meet Penelope Cruz?" It's the girl with the hair. Her friend lingers alongside, so I know the entire changing room is listening in.

I pull out my school tracksuit, avoiding eye contact.

"Only once. She wanted Dad to design a house shaped like a vial of blood, three floors of it underground. With blood coloured glass, lit from below, all the way down." I cross my fingers, acting as if the whole subject is so boring, a technique I learned from Bethany; it ALWAYS got her the attention she wanted. "Can't remember why it fell through."

"Cool," says the tall one, with a flick of her hair. "I'm Alice and this is Megan.

I am IN.

It only turns out that Bully Boy, aka Dim Thug aka Warthog – his real name is Aloysius which explains A LOT

31

– is the son of the Principal who pretends to be friendly but is really strict and heavy with the school rules and regulations. This is NOT good news. I have a lifetime ahead of me in this school that I would really prefer to survive.

Warthog and I are bound to be paired by some well-meaning teacher in a science experiment and I'll probably end up blind.

I feel pretty flat when Flicky Girl – sorry, *Alice* tells me about him but I pretend not to care. Trouble is, secretly I hoped Eva was right. That maybe here, in a new school, in a new country, where nobody knows anything about me… maybe here I could be whoever I wanted to be. As invisible as a sea monkey in a 50 metre pool. I might even make friends for life.

But then, as I walk out towards the sports field, something miraculous happens that is totally REAL. Okay, well maybe it's just pretty cool, ice freezer filled with frozen yoghurt cool, but it is absolutely the best thing in AGES. Who's waiting with his buddies to taunt me? (Well, okay, the first bit's bad but it is SO worth it.) Only the red-headed earwig himself, Aloysius Darcy, with his little bully-buds. I guess I'm the new easy target or he's looking for revenge for this morning. I can see them coming forward to block the path with him in the lead.

At least it's not Laura they're picking on, I think and steel myself to pretend I haven't seen them and to stroll nonchalantly past when this girl passes between me and Bully Boy.

"Zip's down," she says, casual as you like.

He looks down – he has to – and it isn't, so everyone laughs. At him, not me. She waits for me to catch up. "I'm Abby," she says, pushing her glasses up her nose.

"Jessie."

And then she's gone, out onto the track.

SIX

Laura is late out from Homework Club, which gives me time to catalogue my first day. Nobody can say I haven't made an impression.

I have…

1. Crumpled the Principal.
2. Who, in turn, spilt coffee copiously on a teacher I have for at least two classes a day.
3. Been humiliated in front of the whole school at assembly. (Well, okay, *that* wasn't my fault entirely.)
4. *Accidentally* lied to my entire class about knowing A-list celebrities.
5. Made an arch-enemy of the Principal's son.
6. Made a new friend, maybe?

Whatever happened to keeping my head down and blending in? It's only a matter of time before everyone finds out I've never even crossed the street within sight of a Z-list celebrity, at which point it will all get worse than waking up

34

to find a rat peeing into your ear.

A thin drizzle nudges me in under the lip of the door of Laura's school. I stare up at the sky, hoping for a distraction but I can't make anything out beyond 'rain cloud', 'another, bigger rain cloud' and 'almost a rain cloud'.

It's as if Irish clouds don't 'do' shapes.

Of course, Laura being Laura has had the most fantastic day ever. She has *the* best teacher – "no joking, she's AMAZING!" – and guess what? Ms O'Brien used to be a nun. "Or she wanted to be but then she fell in love but she didn't tell us that, that was Caroline who wants to be my BEST FRIEND forever and a day and maybe blood brothers but I dunno if girls can be blood brothers. She says they can in Ireland?"

The wind keeps flicking her veil into my face. I'm about to try a 'snatch n destroy' mission when a breathless Abby tailgates us.

"Phew. Thought I'd missed you."

She's grinning in a way that's impossible to resist. The sun comes out, Laura's veil explodes into fairy dust and I'm freewheeling out the school gate and onto the street if I've lived here all my life. Maybe Eva was right cos get this, not only is Abby in my class, not only did she defend me against Alo the Ignoramus but she lives on my street!

~ ~ ~

Abby tells me everything I need to know about St Brigid's. There's so much arm-waving that she must sometimes take off and fly into the trees. Apparently she meant to fill me in

35

at lunch time but couldn't find me. (I was checking up on Laura. See, I'm not all bad.)

"Alice, the one who quizzed you?" I nod. "NOT sweet. And I don't mean in a nice way, as if she's the Corpse Bride or anything. I mean as in a jackal's not sweet or a spit-bomb." Abby hits the button to cross the road with a sequence of taps. I'm guessing it's meant to make the lights change faster. "Says, 'E-ewe' a lot, so she probably should be called The Sheep. I was going to suggest it last term but being new and all and it seemed unfair on sheep."

"You're new too?"

"Came with Dad. Part of the job lot. There was a big row about Dad hauling the pagoda and cherubs along. Mum hates them but Dad's dad built them or something so even we lived in a tent, He'd find a place for them."

According to Abby, a ginormous number of people would LOVE to shove Alice/The Sheep/Flicky Monster down a rabbit hole. "'Cept she'd be sure to pop back up and be, like, five times taller with even sharper elbows and fangs." It's not a pretty image. "But she's also a bit dim so apart from holding grudges – and making them up – elbowing you out of queues and blanking you, that's pretty much her entire arsenal."

I can't keep up. Abby uses 56 words where five would do and I love it but I'm so busy listening, I know I'm missing out on heaps. No one talks this fast in California.

"…Course it'd be easier if Dad was an international spy but I don't think Mum could cope with the hours, which are bad enough," she says. "I think that's why she joined, like, every community group she could. So she'd be as busy as him. Plus she hoped it'd help us fit in. Mum's big into fitting in. She's already chairing the Tidy Towns Committee."

Alice's clone is Megan who "really, really tries not to think for herself". Abby shrugs. "She's quite nice underneath, if you get her on her own and there's no-one else around to see her with you. Her parents split up last year. I think it messed her up."

Abby tugs leaves from bushes as we pass the park, dissecting and scattering them like a grim leaf reaper. By then, I have learnt that our school has four acres of grass we're not meant to walk on, three ghosts and a grumpy but occasional poltergeist in the Science Lab. "Story is it's the angry spirit of a frog that was dissected while alive, a monk who was buried there before the school was built or a Victorian girl who disappeared from the house that became the convent and was never found."

It's pretty cool to be going to a haunted school. In L.A. nothing's older than it needs to be and everyone who is old is pretending they're not.

"Either way," says Abby, "it only pinches. "

"For real?"

She shrugs. "Doesn't hurt. Like a teensie electric shock. I think it's lonely. Mind you," she grins in a way that could be demonic if you were afraid of her, "when it happened to Alice she was in with the nurse for half an hour and had to be sent home for nerves. Maybe she has weird magnetic skin or something."

"Or she wanted to bail on Science?"

"I guess we *were* cutting up a heart." We're heading up the hill, With her nails, she carves a leery face into a particularly thick leaf and hands it to Laura who holds it like an icon the rest of the way home. "But I kind of liked it. Is that weird?"

"No," I say, meaning *absolutely*. "What else?"

"I tried to get everyone to call O'Flaherty *The OOF*, on account of her first name's Orla but it didn't catch. Now she's The Exorcist on account of she teaches religion. Used to be a nun."

"Is every teacher an ex-nun?"

"In secondary, only her. You can tell by the way she walks." She shimmies ahead, by way of explanation, nothing moving but her feet, all in a steady flow. "It's called *gliding*. As if they're hovering just above the ground."

Instantly, I remember the look on Ms O'Flaherty's face when the coffee flew through the air. She jumped back and knocked over the potted plant. "She wasn't gliding this morning." (Didn't I mention the plant? Well, there was a lot going on and it was a prickly sort of plant so I felt bad.)

I never get to explain the joke cos Laura interrupts to tell Abby about her visions.

"*Versions*," I whisper, pulling Abby ahead, as if this explains everything since Abby's too polite *not* to talk to my IRRITATING kid sister. "Versions of stories. Ghost stories. Lives of Saints. Laura's mad about stories that feature the Virgin Mary and a motorbike. Dad says not to encourage her or she'll start talking to imaginary people and thinking she wants to be a goat."

We both turn to look at the poor deluded innocent.

"What?" says Laura. "What?!"

SEVEN

Abby lives next door.

Not down the road or up the drainpipe or alongside. She lives in the very other half of our semi-detached house. A happy little bubble explodes in my noggin: I have a new best friend who lives next door! It's on the tip of my tongue to ask her in… But here's the snag. Dad's standing at the top of the stairs in a pencil skirt modelling a cerise top for Eva's opinion.

I've told him over and over. He hasn't the knees for a pencil skirt.

Abby's behind me waiting for the invite that she knows has to be coming when I pull the door nearly closed again to block the view. "See you Monday!" I say, as if I was never asking her in.

As if this is perfectly normal behaviour for someone who has just met the best friend she's likely to meet. EVER.

"Okay," says Abby and trots next door.

I know it's rude and the worst thing I could do to a friend who so recently saved me from UTTER HUMILIATION because if she had a tail, it would be tucked between her legs. She doesn't even cut across the grass. She follows the path to her hall door through their perfect lawn even though NO-ONE is looking but us. Laura's no help.

"Why can't Abby come in?" she says, sweeping her veil over her shoulder. "Isn't she your friend?"

"Want to call for me on Monday?"

"Sure!" The tail Abby doesn't have starts wagging again but I feel awful. I push past Laura into the kitchen and grab an apple from the fridge.

"You should be nice to your friends. If she were my friend I'd invite her in."

One of these days Laura WILL grow up and I'll tell her how annoying she was. Better still, I'll be ten times more annoying back though she'll probably still be more irritating than I will ever manage to be to her. I could try *embarrassing*. Heaven knows, I've learnt from the Two Geniuses of Embarrassing: her and Dad. I'll wear a Godzilla suit to her wedding. I'll snog her first boyfriend. I'll–

"Aren't you bringing your friend in?" says Dad, appearing behind me. Like an echo.

Great. That helps. He's thrown jeans on, as if that makes the cerise top okay and come downstairs expecting to greet my new friend. "Homework," I say, guzzling the longest glass of water. "Lots and lots of homework. Abby's very serious about her homework."

"I imagine she would be," he says, which isn't a nice thing to say about any girl in Second Year, 'especially when it isn't true and I only made it up cos I couldn't bring her in because my dad wasn't looking dad-like.

"It's a tarty top," I throw in passing and, when he doesn't react, "It's a stupid colour *AND* your knees are UGLY."

"I like it," says Laura.

"You're always saying I should wear more colour!" says Dad. Grrr.

I grab my bag from the hall and stomp upstairs so he'll know I'm mad. All 14 stairs I stomp and not a peep from behind me. Not a shout up after me to ask if anything's wrong or if I'm alright. He doesn't even leave the kitchen! Why do I bother? He only ever puts my stomping down to heavy feet or growing up or not knowing my own strength, as if I were a baby clog-wearing dinosaur.

What's the point of having a best friend next door if you have to arrange in advance for your dad to be somewhere else or at least not in women's clothes when they call?

I know it's not his fault. That's what makes it so bad. I've changed out of the hideous uniform and into my skinny jeans when he knocks and comes in to ask what I fancy for tea. It has to be something with sausages, apparently. Because he missed Irish sausages so much, he's bought a fridge-ful. The room takes on a gruesome shade of pink.

"What's the story?" I manage. "Have they sacked you already?"

"Funny girl. If you want to know, I told the Boss I had to work from home today and afternoons next week." He beams, like a cat that has found the litter tray but thinks it's a sandpit full of buried mice. "Said I needed to be here to welcome my gorgeous daughters home from their new school."

He looks so proud that he stood up for himself. It's hard to be mad.

"There's no need," I say. "Eva's here."

"You and I know you are not going to see Eva hovering around to welcome you home anytime soon." It's true. She's not the homemaking sort, especially this close to a show. "It's a win-win. I get to play mother to my lovely muses while my lovely lady completes her work without being harassed for merely mortal things such as food and drink and conversation."

"Sorry for being a grump."

"Hey, I love my little grump. Beats being a Grinch. Or a Chihuahua." I hate it when parents are nice. I hate it that he wanted to be here for us when all I wanted was to be able to fling the door open and invite my new friend in. It's SO frustrating.

"Laura's right. It looks okay. That colour," I mutter, waving at a nosey neighbour in the house opposite. She waves straight back before she cops on that she has been RUMBLED.

There's a flake of mascara on Dad's nose. I reach up to wipe it off as Laura trots in. "It's harder to apply than it looks," he says. I nod as if I don't know. I stuck the brush in my eye the first time I tried. Twice. "You'd think I'd be handy at it by now."

Dad wears women's clothes cos they feel right. As if he's a woman *and* a man or a man who *sometimes* wants to be a woman. And yes, it should be weird but I can't remember Dad when he didn't. Sometimes it's even fun, like having a big grown up doll to dress. He's still my frustrating Dad underneath, the one who dances jigs around the kitchen on a Monday morning to try and cheer us up when I can barely cope with silence.

"Coach said I can try out for the school team," I say, as if it's nothing special. Knowing it'll please him to skinny bits. "Only for the reserves cos it's mid season but–"

He grins and I'm up in the air being spun.

"Yihoo! Did you hear that Laura? My little girl is going to be the next Rugby World Champ!"

"Aaagh! Enough! Dad!"

Okay, it's fun so long as I don't hit my ankles off the wall or Laura's head. Well, okay, if they hit Laura's head, she might stop wanting to be a nun which is okay, but there's very little chance. She's an expert at ducking.

"They're good, y'know. Top of the league last two years!" He puts me down with sudden purpose. "I'll coach you! We'll go down to the park and practice. We need to work on your throwing. See if you don't make Captain before the season's out!"

"I'm not that good, Dad."

"Who's the coach? Maybe I know him?" Dad hasn't played for decades but he still thinks he must know everyone.

"He's Brazilian."

"Called Jesus," pipes Laura. "I like this school."

"That's great, Pumpkin. I don't see us moving for a very long time."

"It's pronounced *Hey-Sooos*," I explain.

I'll make it up to Abby on Monday. Find a story that makes me not asking her in seem quirky or sweet. Say Dad suffers from Fear of School Friends or that he'd been bingeing on chocolate and I needed to hide the evidence before Eva came in from the studio. I'll think of something.

I always do.

"So, Sausage n Mash or Toad in the Hole?"

"Toad in the Hole!" pipes Laura. "It's Jessie's favourite."

Sometimes I just love my family to bits but I still growl at her and ask her what she wants in return as soon as Dad's gone. Which is how I come to spend the next half hour testing her on the lives of saints and who got martyred in which disgusting way.

Sometimes life's too short to have a saintly sister.

EIGHT

I lied about the homework.

The teachers all took pity on us, except for The Exorcist. She set us a gazillion verbs to conjugate that all seem to have something to do with falling, running and causing accidents. When I'm done, I head up onto the Cloud Platform with a few Tootsie Rolls so I can pretend I'm somewhere else. Of course I wanted to see more of Gramma and Gaffa but I didn't know that the sky in Ireland would be full of shapeless grey clouds that do nothing but piggyback all day long. Today, there isn't even a hint of blue seeping through.

A little blue would be nice.

A cloud shaped like a big thumbs-up or an American flag or a Hershey's kiss would be spectacular.

I can just about make out a face in on section of the sky, but it's a faint and lumpy one.

See, I *liked* L.A. but I LOVED California. The weather and the colours, the sounds and the smells. But what I hate most about moving this time is that everyone in my old school probably assumes that we ran away because of what happened. I'd love to spray paint it all over the school walls: *Bethany, You Did Not Drive Me Away.*

Laura and I have been in lots of schools, following Dad's work around and something similar to what happened with Bethany has happened in different ways in every one. If we'd let people like Bethany drive us away, we'd have left America years ago.

Dad appears with a glass of iced peppermint tea. "Dinner'll be ready in ten." He sits down sideways on the instep. Peppermint tea is my favourite drink; tonight it tastes medicinal.

He squints up at the sky.

All I can think of is maybe it'll rain properly. At least then some of the grey clouds would have to disappear.

"What about that? Face with a big nose?"

I shrug and Buffy climbs off my lap for a good stretch. "The clouds… they're different here."

"How was your first day really?"

"I waltzed with the Principal, blew kisses to a bully, told everyone you used to be engaged to Penelope Cruz." And slammed the door on my new and only friend, but I don't say that. I've been mean enough to him today.

"Same old?"

"Same old."

"It'll get easier," he says, squeezing my shoulder and sneezing again as Buffy strolls over him and into the house. "You're just not fluent in Irish-cloud-speak yet. Laura says your friend lives next door?"

I nod.

"That's a good start?"

"Yeah." The face in the clouds grows a nose that could have inhaled Bethany and all her hair. I point it out to Dad. "An ant-eater."

"Why so it is!"

I remember the baby that's coming and hug him so tight.

"What's that for? Not that I'm complaining but... You're not crying?"

He pulls me back to arm's length to check if I'm okay and I smile up at him. If I find the right reason for Abby not to come here, there's no reason we can't hang out at hers! I mean, my house isn't exactly exciting. We don't have Wiis or X-Boxes or anything like that. Eva n Dad don't cook fancy cakes or buy in lots of junk so even if I have her over some day when Dad's at work, she'll probably suggest her house every time after that.

The magical thing that makes everything okay now is that all through the Bethany debacle and the move, Eva's baby was there, starting. I'm pretty sure it will be the cutest little baby and probably not annoying at all, unlike Laura.

That makes me feel fine again.

So long as we're all together, does it matter where we live?

More importantly at this moment in time, will the new baby look like Laura or me?

~ ~ ~

There is NOTHING nicer to eat than Dad's Toad in the Hole. He shapes the sausage meat into little rugby balls before he pours the batter over. Sometimes, like tonight, he drizzles sautéed onion and cheese on top. On St Patrick's Day last year, he dyed the sausages green only they turned kind of purple and the batter took on a luminous nuclear glow. We ate it wearing dark glasses.

"But they make wonderful pets," says Dad, while he serves up toads. I like the way he thinks, mostly, but this is plain weird.

"We're getting a toad?"

"Ant-eater," says Dad, with a grin as if I'm in on the plan. Now I know what he's at! Eva should be glad I didn't see a hippo in the clouds but she's having none of it. "We are not getting an ant-eater."

"Apparently, they make really affectionate pets and you know how you hate ants…" He winks at me and Laura.

"We'll buy a spray," says Eva. "You haven't gone and brought one without telling me?"

"Course not."

"Ants have souls too," says Laura.

"No they don't." Sometimes you have to squish your little sister quickly. "No more than piranha fish do."

"Do too."

"Don't!"

"GIRLS!" shouts Eva, turning to Dad: "And we are not getting an ant-eater!"

"Okay," says Dad, grinning like a fox. "How about a dog?"

"We have a fish and a cat and I have you," says Eva. "Surely that's enough for now?"

Which is when I realise that if Abby lives next door, Jennifer must be her Mum. This is okay. Not great, but fine. But it also means Abby's is also most likely related to the man who pruned himself out of a tree last night while ogling Eva and Dad in the garden.

This could get messy.

~ ~ ~

First thing after breakfast, Dad and I escape to his new office. Bright sky. Fluffy but shapeless clouds. It's nice to get away from all the boxes and the '*what goes where*' of it. Not to mention Laura's excitement at rediscovering all the things she'd packed as if they were magical talismen.

His office is near the docks; high up, full of glass and sharp angles. He's been working on his first commission, a design for a new crematorium, since they offered him the job two months ago and he wants me to have a look. Often, I see things he's missed or hasn't thought about; makes us both feel good.

I'm looking for paperweights to hold the plans flat on his desk when a baldy man in pinstripe and swagger slaps Dad on the back. "What's this, Frank? Working on a Saturday!? Marriage falling apart already?"

He has an enormously ugly moustache, one in which you could easily hide squirrels. Except that the squirrels would complain. Loudly. They'd probably spit stale acorns at your ears when you turned away. He sees me and holds out a hand.

"You must be Bessie."

"Jessie." For a boomy man, it's a limp handshake.

"Had an odd aunt called Bessie. Became a writer. Your

49

dad's boss, Matt O'Grady, that's lucky me. Can't wait to see the plans, Frank! Lot of people waiting on them. Huge excitement!" And then he's gone in an ectoplasm of floral aftershave. "Nice to see you so keen!"

Dad has based his crematorium design on Newgrange, this Neolithic tomb up in the Boyne Valley that we have visited when I was little, before Laura, but I only remember it from photos. "Rumour has it, some of the passage graves were used as birthing chambers too," he says. "That's why it's relevant. It's making death part of the cycle of life; less scary."

I love Dad's plans. They may only be lines on a page, but I can really visualise the spaces, as if I were walking through the rooms in my head. I think it's built into my DNA; probably the gene that replaced the popularity one. "Should the washrooms be above the ovens? Mightn't they smell of smoke?"

"Oh the smoke will be filtered out," Dad says, "but a good point. Anything else?"

"Sliding doors. People who are upset shouldn't need to work out whether to push or pull. Less chance of accidentally walloping a Great Aunt. What are the gardens like?"

"You need spaces people can be alone in, even for a moment. To reflect or pull themselves together before they face everyone else. And some place for children so they don't get overwhelmed."

Dad says I have the makings of an awesome architect. That's pretty cool.

"We'll set up our own firm," I say. "Keane & Keane, Father

and Child Genius, sorry, *Daughter*. Creative Architects of Grand Design." Normally, this is where we sort of whoop in a grown up way and hatch out our ideal empire; offices in every major city, at the top of the tallest buildings, tickling clouds.

But this time, Dad rolls up his plans and goes sort of thoughtful. He doesn't contradict me and he doesn't look sad or flattened but he looks out the window for the longest time. As if he hadn't heard. It must be the jet lag. Gaffa said we'd be bog rats for days.

"Be cool, wouldn't it, Dad? You n me, being a family firm?"

"Yeah," he says quietly, ruffling my hair. This usually makes me growl but he's gone so quiet, as if he's somewhere else entirely.

"Is something wrong, Dad?"

"No. Nothing. Course not," he says, staring back out over the river at the city unravelling into the distance. He doesn't look right; like an extra in a movie who hasn't been told where to stand.

Suddenly I feel as tired as dishwater. "Can we go home now?"

NINE

"All I'm saying is it'd be better for Laura not to talk about her visions in school."

"Why?" says Laura, all butter-wouldn't-melt. We live ten minutes from school but she has been hovering by the kitchen door for 20 minutes with her little pink rucksack and veil. Dad won't let her go alone yet and this really bugs her. Plus I am the ONLY one who knows Laura is super-annoying. Everyone else thinks she's cute as several little buttons tied on a ribbon around a rabbit's neck.

"I saw her in the yard telling people." Laura gives me daggers but it's water off my scaly back. What are kid sisters for if not to aggravate? It's not as if I have much power over anything else in my life. "Everyone's talking about it."

"Everyone?" Grrr. Dad can be so ANNOYING sometimes.

"*Everyone* who has someone in the little school."

"It's not little," says the freak who is my sister. "It's a bigger school than yours."

Time for the Concerned Older Sister angle: "Dad, I

don't want people to laugh at her." Giving him my best Troubled Look, I stick out my tongue at Laura behind his back as the doorbell goes. "I'd *hate* to see her hurt."

"Oh, I don't know," says Dad, going to answer the door. "She seems able to handle it."

"People always make fun of saints," says Laura, as if this makes it alright for her to turn our family into a laughing stock.

"Yeah, well you're not a saint yet, 'less I missed some new miracle… Like you were garrotted or hanged or torn in four or something."

Enter Abby stage left with Dad; okay, from the hall, but it's still dramatic. Fortunately Dad's still in his pjs and dressing gown; if it is a bit flouncier than most men's dressing gowns, it's only the fluffy slippers that really give the game away but she seems in more of a hurry to get out of there than I am so I don't think she has noticed.

"Ready?"

I nod, grab my coat and somehow we are out before Laura, which is an achievement.

"What's the rush?"

"Want to walk to school with Alo?"

Perfect. He lives on our road. Lots of opportunity to bump into one of the few people in the whole wide world that I'd rather avoid. Laura speeds past, her veil wriggling ALMOST as much as her wiggly bum. It does wiggle. Not even sure I know how she moves forward really; so much of her body is going from side to side instead. It's very un-nun-like, so I like it and haven't passed comment yet. Good to have something in reserve in the Annoy Kid Sister box.

We speed down the hill towards the park. "Which house?"

Abby points back the way we came, which is strange.

"So he's a neighbour?" I get this feeling I'm not going to like the answer.

She shrugs her bag onto her other shoulder. "Alo's my brother."

I'm not surprised she's on the team, despite being a good two inches shorter than me. We catch up with Laura at the lights. "But Alo's in our class," I start and then it dawns on me with a horrifying rush of blood to the head. "No! You're—"

"Twins, yup."

How spooky is that? My best friend and the world's nastiest specimen of boy-hog shared a womb. I feel queasy, as if I'd swallowed a handful of worms and they'd be all gone off. Bad enough sharing a womb with a boy, but to share it with Alo!

"So he's, like, your evil twin?!" Laura always listens when she shouldn't. "Do you hear each other's thoughts? Can you read his mind? Do you share dreams?"

"No, no and no," says Abby, laughing.

"That means your dad—?"

"Yup."

Snail slime, even when scrubbed from fabric, shows up under phosphorescent light. I have a feeling there's a snail-slime target drawn invisibly on my back. We cross the road only when the little green man does his gig, even with Alo on our tail. No jay-walking cos Laura's with us and we have to set a good example.

"Sorry," says Abby.

Past the butchers, bakers and lingerie. Not all in the same shop. That would be gross; weird gross and kind of sick. There's a cafe further down but we turn down a side road to the school before then. "You don't have an uncle living with you?" She shakes her head, puzzled. "Adult male cousin, loony vicar, goofy tree-hugger?"

"Why?"

"No reason."

So there you have it. I meet the one person I think I can *really* be best friends with and her brother is the school psycho. Not only that, but the guy who was staring at my dad dancing in a dress with my step-mum, is not *only* the father of best friend but my *School Principal.* The guy I planted into the lino on my first day at *his* school.

I am officially doomed.

Dad doesn't need to muck up my new life. I'm doing exceptionally well all by myself at breakneck speed. "About Friday." It's time to confront the hippo in the room. "Sorry for not asking you in only Eva, she doesn't like strangers in the house when she's finishing work for a show."

"Cos she thinks they'll leak to the press what she's making?"

"No." I hadn't thought of that. "Well I don't think so. More to do with her energy field getting disrupted." Sorry Eva but you can get really odd around this time. "She's like a lioness, y'know and the installations are her cubs."

"So her show is about wild animals?"

"Depends on how you classify 'wild'." I'm beating about

the bush with a hairbrush and it isn't working. "I mean, *we're* wildlife to lions!"

"Nah," says Abby. "We're food."

"Anyway," I yank myself back on track as we turn down the lane leading to the school gate. "She doesn't want us having anyone over. Dad says she's worried she might accidently fling them into the kiln or make them model nude for her. (I have no idea where that came from!) Even Dad's pretty much invisible to her at this stage." I need to stop this now. It's not fair to Eva.

"S'okay," she says. "Must be cool to have an artist for a Mum."

Which is how I find myself explaining about Mum dying and Eva coming along. That now it's as if Eva were our mother, mostly, cos, like, Laura doesn't even remember Mum.

"But that's terrible," Abby says, wrapping her arm around my shoulder. "I can't imagine what it would be like to lose Mum. I mean, she drives me demented, especially when she's trying to 'show an interest.' And I know she means well but it's SOOOO awkward when she asks about boys." She catches my look and nods.

"And don't *talk* to me about the advice! *'Remember, you're in charge. Don't let any boy do anything'.* As if I would. I mean, boys, they're not exactly adorable, though I guess Mr Byrne is cute in a Gryffindor sort of way."

Abby takes a deep breath; it's amazing how few of them she needs to keep the words flowing. Dad hasn't tried to give any advice yet. For a guy who wears dresses and stockings, he is UTTERLY uncomfortable with the whole *me turning into a woman* thing. "Byrne is History. You haven't had him yet." Then we belly-dive into the pond that is our daily wormhole of school. "But I couldn't imagine not having her around to do those things."

I feel like a TOAD.

Not only have I lied but Abby has been REALLY kind and nice about it. Even if I kissed a prince who wasn't repulsive and if I was actually willing to kiss him, I'd still be a toad. While I'm thinking about this, Abby suddenly steers me in the opposite direction to avoid Alice and her cronies. I trip over someone's bag, do an unintentional pixie dance and right myself as The Gorgeous Boy turns around.

"Hey," he says. "You found your classroom then?" It's as if a thousand songbirds had dragged the sun out from behind the clouds to shine SPECIFICALLY on me! Okay, so it's a bit obvious but sweet too, as if he wanted to find something to say to me.

I manage a nod and he's gone.

"At least warn me when you're going to push me in a different direction," I hiss at Abby, who grins in that impossible way as if she'd planned it all along. (She didn't. Abby's short-sighted. It's a miracle she makes it into the right class every day, she says.) Anyway, she says his name's Jason and he lives with two uncles who run a catering firm.

"Always dashing off to help out with events and floods his pores with aftershave so he won't smell of onions," she says but I think he smells DIVINE.

Divine for a boy that is. I daydream though Geography without despairing that I'll ever recall all the Irish rivers. The only Irish river I learnt the name of in L.A. was the Shannon because a classmate had the same name. 'Cept we called her The Shining on account of she had this look that could freeze you in your tracks.

On this uniquely GOLDEN day, I don't get shouted at, ticked off or picked on once. I manage to avoid Alo, getting quizzed about *My Life With Hollywood Stars* and tripping over anything or anyone else all day.

My luck expires when I run onto the pitch after school to try out for the school's rugby team. "What's wrong? Afraid you'll get a little bwuisy on your shoulder?" Yup, any kudos I had earned for having met Tom Cruise evaporates the minute they see my American kit. Which would be bad enough if Dad had NOT insisted on buying the kit *without me* six months ago.

"Ooooh look, it's Super-Girl."

See, Dad decided to buy me a kit that was two sizes too large so I could "grow into it". Long before the comments start – witty as they are – I feel like a padded Buddha.

"Oh please don't beat me up. You look so big and stwong."

I say nothing, only focus my embarrassment, humiliation and anger at the opposition and play like I've never played before. Then I throw a tackle, elbow Alo into a puddle the colour and texture of cow poo and push through to the base line, shredding my opponents like wheat.

SCORE!

I AM cool.

TEN

For once, I am truly glad to see Dad when we get in. Laura's in an Armageddon of a grump from having to hang out at the side of the pitch waiting for me. "I'm on the team. Well, not really but I'm on the reserves which means practice after school twice a week and matches on Sunday."

"Slow down, Squirrel! Give me a chance to hug you."

Dad's hugs are almost as good as Gramma's. Also, he hasn't paid any attention to Laura giving out about how BORING it is to stand watching STUPID people push other STUPID people into the mud and how it's like "some gross out reality game played in poop". He's in a twin-set – nicer than it sounds – pale turquoise skirt and cardigan, with a cream blouse and he's still tanned so it works. No pearls. At least he knows not to try pearls.

"Well?" says Dad. "Tell me more!"

Peeved, Laura thumps off upstairs. It's on the tip of my tongue to shout after her that maybe she should pray for a better mood but I resist the temptation.

"Coach hinted that if he could, he'd have me on pitch

but we're already mid-season." Before I can finish the sentence, Dad swears that he WILL get me on that pitch, even if it means we do extra coaching every night.

"Just let me get this crematorium in first."

~ ~ ~

I lynch Buffy from Fish Watch and steal her upstairs with me. Buffy's my homework aide: she keeps my lap warm – an achievement in this country – and if I try to get up cos I'm bored, she digs her claws into me. That kind of persuades me to stay and get the homework done.

There are three goldfish left in the tank with Ponchinello, because Laura now feeds him constantly. Mostly worms (dug up in the dark; the best time, apparently), flies, beetles and the odd small apple which makes his poo float.

They are very fit but anxious little goldfish on account of having to swim very quickly into the tiny rock cave when Ponchinello remembers he's hungry again. I can't look. Too much like a watery coliseum where the lion has scales.

~ ~ ~

Eco Living. The project is due next Monday. Laura is the only person I know who enjoys homework. Dad says I was the same until I turned nine and discovered it wouldn't make me grow taller faster. 700 words and all I can think of is: "Go live in a hot climate. Then you won't waste natural energy resources or fabric. Switch to cold drinks to avoid the endless boiling of kettles for cups of tea nobody drinks." I have a sneaky feeling this is NOT what Mr Lynch is looking for.

"Jessie, your friend's here!"

Before Eva can finish saying, "I'll send her up," I'm in the hall. Not quite ready for her to see Dad in a twin-set *just* yet. (More like EVER.)

"Mum says you can come over."

"Great! See yah!" I shout back, closing the door tightly behind me.

Abby leads the way through the arch. "If she asks, we're working on the Eco Living project," she says.

Fine with me.

~ ~ ~

Abby's room is like nothing I've seen in real life. Her duvet cover matches the pillowcase and the walls, almost. The ornaments aren't dusty or cracked and there isn't even a lost sock up among them. Mind you, there is also a 'Duty Roster' on the landing, which is her father's idea, as is the Homework Log in which Abby has to write down the time she spends daily on each subject.

"Where does Alo sleep?" Abby points upwards at the attic. That makes sense. "And not cos he really IS a manmade monster, created from a lump of contaminated poo?"

"Alo's not that bad," says Abby, unpacking her schoolbag. "Sometimes he can be very sweet."

She's saying that out of loyalty. Unless she and Alo really are the opposite of me and Laura. See everyone thinks Laura's cute but I *know* she's irritating. So Abby thinks Alo is sweet while I know him to be the tall spawn of Satan.

We flip open her Geography book just before Abby's

mum arrives with carrot sticks, hummus and a few vegetable crisps, "to stimulate your brain cells". This is how Mums are MEANT to be. Okay so hummus is about as tasty as squished brain with all the flavour and colour taken out but I love the IDEA that she would do this. "Hope you're not just chatterboxing?"

"Charging along Mrs D.," says I. "It's great to have a study buddy."

She wrinkles her nose. I don't think she likes the sound of a study buddy. We put our heads down. Soon as the door closes behind her, Abby writes '30 minutes' and 'Eco Project' into the Homework Log, props a chair against the door – her "early warning system" – and drags out an old biscuit tin from under her bed. Make-up. Tons of make-up.

"Want a go?" she says, tying her hair back so she can start her transformation.

"I'm okay for now."

Abby squints at the mirror and starts to apply shadow. Can't be easy, being short-sighted. "I suppose you had to leave lots of friends behind in L.A.?"

"A few." I don't want her to think I'm a loser. "But I have a cat now. She's called Buffy."

"Nice. We had to leave ours in Mayo. She was pretty old and Dad said they don't like being uprooted. A neighbour took her in but Mum said she had, like, five different homes anyway. Mum cooked roasts to make sandwiches for Dad so she always came home. Cats can smell meat roasting through a whole estate. Once winter comes and Mum starts her roasts again, we'll probably get found by another cat."

"What was her name?"

"Gruffalo. She was dead grumpy! What do you think?"

Her eye is a perfect bruise, the most realistic black eye ever. "Cool."

"I'm better at scars and I do a mean bullet hole, in case you ever want to dress up as Bambi's Mum." As Abby wipes it off, I tell her about the baby but swear her to secrecy. We spend half an hour thinking of names from the weird to the wonderful while she starts again, conventional make up this time.

"So long as they don't call the baby Jedward or Bieber," says Abby. "Want me to give you a scar?"

"Nah. Thanks. Anyway, it might be a girl."

"Not a chance. Jet lag turns them into boys. Well known fact." She turns to me. "So, do I look 18?"

So then, as I do with Dad, I fix Abby's mascara, tone down the eye shadow and replace her lippy with a quieter shade. "Now you do."

"Wow! Where did you learn to do that?!"

~ ~ ~

The very next day, I'm in the queue behind Jason, waiting for the Library to open. Not wanting to be pushy, I don't say anything. Besides, I'm totally tongue-tied again, as in my tongue just dive-bombed into a series of acrobatic loops and knots that even a Scout with badges up and down her sleeves would find impossible.

But it's okay. He spots me and says, 'Hey'. It's a warm 'hey', so I say, 'Hey' back and then he asks if I've fallen over lately. From him, it doesn't annoy me half as much as it would if anyone else said it. I mean, he knew me before I became a teacher-felling dork.

I don't even mind that everyone in the corridor is looking at us until Alice and a bunch of girls come thundering along and surround him with noise so I head off, forgetting completely to drop in my application form for a library card. Which had been the whole point of queuing.

Do I care?

Absolutely and definitively and zoomiliciously NOT.

ELEVEN

Friday.

The last day of the second-longest week of my life. I feel I can take a deep breath and relax, despite Dad making porridge. Bethany masterminded my first-longest but that was in a different country so I've decided to obliterate that memory along with water slides, soggy asparagus and Dad's one and only (phew!) attempt at belly dancing.

"Dad? You will have to work in the office next week, right?" This might not *exactly* say, 'It was really lovely having you here when we came home every day and having all your care and attention', but he knows. He's my dad.

"Sure," he says and looks disappointed. Okay, well he *should* know.

"It's just... that your new job, it's important. And exciting. Isn't the crematorium due soon? Also, can we go to town tonight to get proper kit for the match on Sunday?"

"Bell bell BELL!" Laura has decided that shouting this when the bell goes will annoy me. I'm pretending not to notice and so is Dad but it's hard. She's done it every day this week in protest at watching me play rugby.

"We can do that tomorrow."

"I was hoping to catch up on Maths tomorrow. I'm way behind." I put on my best Innocent Face. See, the plan is to hang out with Abby on Saturday. She says if we go to town, she can show me the cool shops for comics and clothes and we can talk about Jason.

After three nights of running back over every gesture, pause and word of our last exchange, I'm not sure he wanted to be waylaid by Alice and the gang. Did he seem slightly helpless? Does that mean I'm the one to rescue him?

Expecting Abby, I swill the remainder of my porridge down the sink while Dad answers the door to her but then I hear this man's voice, offering us a lift.

"Since it must have been a long week for the girls–"

I follow Laura out and see Abby, which is good. We grin. Then I see Alo, disguised as a butter-wouldn't-melt brother and tuck the grin away in favour of a frown. Worst of all, their dad is beaming at mine. It's as if the world has skidded to a stop and caught us all.

"That's very thoughtful of you."

"George," says Mr D. and they shake hands.

In that one frozen moment I see everything Abby's dad must see in sharp focus. Dad's furry pink slippers. Laura's veil. *Ulysses* holding our coats. AND he's peering around Dad as if expecting someone else to emerge from the kitchen. Oh God, please don't let him fancy Eva cos that would just be soooo messy.

Dad's still talking, oblivious. "Great for her to have made

friends so quickly…" I grab Laura, nod to Abby to follow and we are OUT the door, leaving Dad to try and explain. "Oh I guess they want to walk today."

Abby tags on quick as an eel and we don't look back. I just about hear Dad telling Mr D. that walking is such healthy exercise.

~ ~ ~

In Science we're dissecting frogs. In History, it's the Civil War which is a bit of an oxymoron; how can you be *at war* and *civil*? Having only studied American history, I'm now expected to know who Michael Collins is and the stick insect De Valera, both of whom seem to be old friends to Abby and the rest. Spanish is dandy. I'm way ahead, even if my accent is Mexican.

I'm at my locker working out what books I need for homework when Abby lunges at me with an arm grip that could suffocate a ninja.

"He's coming over!"

"Who is?"

"I'm off to tie my shoelaces or sort out my INCREDIBLY neat locker which means I *will* be watching at a distance to make sure you don't waste the opportunity. Be nice, talk normally, don't say anything daft and get him to ask you out!!" And she's gone as Jason appears.

"Hey," he says.

"Hey." Are we ever going to get past this stage?

"I was wondering if–"

"Sure."

He looks confused. I'm an idiot. He hasn't actually asked me out and I've already said yes. Fortunately, a small bespectacled Second Year arrives giving him no time to react. "Hey, Noodle." Jason cuffs him lightly on the head. "This is Jessie." Noodle nods. I've seen him before but can't think where. "Noodle is my irritating kid brother."

"Every dork should have one," says Noodle.

As they walk off, Noodle swings his bag onto his back. It's as large as a small caravan home. I recognise him now. He's the kid Laura saved. Now if that doesn't give me brownie points…

"Well?" Abby appears like a needle of conscience. "He is DEFINITELY into you. When are you going out?"

"Soon," says I and grin.

~ ~ ~

That evening, when we've bought kit that ACTUALLY fits, Dad takes me into Gramma's favourite store. It's full of little old ladies, sensible heels, displays of expensive bling and handbags. "Mum had a store card. Probably still has. I loved coming here with her. And afterwards, if I was good, we'd share a sticky bun in the restaurant. It's funny but when I come in here," he says, looking around, "it's as if I were that child again."

"Just don't start skipping."

"Skipping? Me?

"Yes. Don't do it."

And he does. Of course he does. Me and my big mouth. Still, it looks funny to see a grown and adulty man skipping and I kind of enjoy the looks he gets. "Enough," I say, in my best Gramma voice, trying not to giggle. "Quieten down or you won't get a sticky bun."

"Half a sticky bun."

"Did you bring Mum here?"

He slips an arm around my shoulders. "I did. Long before you came along. She said the clothes were frumpy. Now, I want your advice on something."

"Have to earn that sticky bun, huh?"

"*Half* a sticky bun."

~ ~ ~

"What do you think?"

"Dad!" I hiss.

"What?" He looks all around to see what I'm hissing about. It's a really beautiful silky red dress that catches the light as it hangs but just beyond the dress, I see Alice and her friend Megan, looking exactly, absolutely and with perfect-sighted eyes our way. What on earth are they doing here?

I smile sweetly at the assistant who has materialised alongside. *This* time the smile fails.

Spectacularly.

"My mum's pregnant," I explain loudly as the girls come into earshot. "And tall. Same height as Dad. Weird, eh? It's okay though, she's our step-mum so we'll just be normal. Size. Eventually." Enough Jessie, stop with the talking, but my mouth just keeps on moving. "Which is good really. Who wants to be monstrous? 'Cept Dad; he LOVES monstrous women!"

"Jessie?" Dad's confused.

"Maternity's over there," says the assistant, pointing left.

"Uh huh," I say and take Dad's arm. "Thanks!" We pass the girls and I know they know. It's Bethany all over again. And Jenny Trump before that. "See yah, Alice, Megan," I say, in passing. As if this were all perfectly normal.

"What was that about?" says Dad. "And how do you know about the baby?"

"I.... guessed?"

"Are you not sleeping again?"

"I don't get up as much as before." Mainly because it's too cold. "But it's okay Dad, I don't feel displaced if that's why you were worried about telling us. I know that's what they say I should feel cos Ms Otis in the old school said that was why I was mean to Laura when I didn't really *intend* to be."

While I rabbit on – anything to forget the look on Alice's face – we've wandered past maternity into the cafe. "But I'm thirteen now. I'm only mean to her cos I want to be and she's a pain. But I think she'll be fine too cos she's mad about babies. I mean look how she is with her freaky fish! I'll make sure she knows it's not a doll and that she can't do things to it."

"You don't think I'm too old?"

"Course not! Lots of kids have elderly parents!" He growls sweetly. "…Who skip through department stores." We hug, with everyone watching and I don't give a DAMN anymore. "A baby's good news. We'll be a real family."

We leave the store full of sticky buns, with two for Laura

and Eva. "'S'pose you'll get married now," I say as we climb into the car. This is a mistake. Dad's a rotten driver when it comes to car parks. He says I distract him but that's just him saving face. It's a boy thing. I check left and right. "Clear. Go. Now." We pull out safely. No honking of horns or whirring of wheels. Smooth.

"I mean, for the baby. Laura n me could be bridesmaids. Then she'd have to get rid of the veil."

"Let's wait and see," he says.

I HATE it when he says that.

"And not a word. Eva wants to tell you both herself, when the time is right."

~ ~ ~

"Dad, this baby...?" I should be asleep but there's this thing niggling me. He looks up over the glasses he uses for close work.

"Yes, love?"

He's making stained glass windows for the crematorium. They even have windowsills but I mustn't get distracted, not if I want to sleep. "You will be a real Dad to it?"

Coming out from behind the table, he gives me a big hug. Note: he really should have put the Stanley knife down first but now's not the time to say.

"Of course I will," he says, softly. "Just as I was for you and Laura."

Much as I love him, this is not exactly reassuring.

71

TWELVE

Next day, I wake up like a bear stuffed into a rucksack that smells off and I take it out on Laura. See, in L.A., we had the tank between us. So long as I didn't peep over or around it and ignored the stench of the algae, I could pretend we had separate rooms.

Eva had us draw a chalk line down the centre of the room; the theory being that we will then respect each other's space. One serious flaw with this: you can *see* over a chalk line.

However, Laura has also promised:

1. Not to pin a veil to my hair while I sleep. The last time, I had a panic attack and swallowed an earplug. *Don't* ask.

2. Not to read prayers at me while I sleep. It's brainwashing and sneaky. I went in to school in L.A. and in front of a whole class recited the Hail Mary instead of asking if I could leave to go to the bathroom.

3. Not to stand at the end of my bed and go
    WOOOO. Granted it was Halloween but she was
    a week early and I KNOW she was pretending to be
    a vision so that I could have had one too, even if it
    was only her and therefore not real.

Is it any wonder I can't sleep sometimes?

I skulk off to the Cloud Platform to puzzle out my mood
after I've fired her shoes back over the chalk line and she's
gone down to complain.

And no, I wasn't ACTUALLY aiming for her. *This* time.
She ducked into the target zone to pick up a pencil. Sucking
slowly on a Sour Patch, I try to figure it out. See, I slept well,
even slept in a little since it's a Saturday but something feels off.

And no, it's nothing to do with Stanley knives or being
smothered by bible-quoting veils, EVEN if that *was* what I
dreamt about. No, it's the sort of bad feeling you get when
you've swallowed something you're allergic to but have to
wait for your arm to explode into boils before you know if
it's going to be fatal.

~ ~ ~

Lunch does nothing to help. Roast chicken, two veg (*no*
spinach aka *spawn-of-Satan*; possibly related to Alo at some
basic genetic level) and roast potatoes. There's even gravy!
Because I don't know who cooked it, I congratulate both
Eva and Dad. This is how you train pets to repeat an activity
you like. "This meal is *wonderful*," I say, kicking Laura under
the table so she chimes in.

"Wonderful," says Laura.

We never have meals like this. Either Dad's been listening to our comments about Gramma's dinners (*Wow, what a fantastic meal! Wish we could eat meals like this every day!*) or something is up.

"More carrots?" says Eva.

"What's with the matching blue dresses?" Laura says as we clear the table. "You're not splitting up?"

"Course not, silly." Dad ruffles her hair while Eva fetches a cake box from the fridge. "Eva, are you going to put them out of their misery?"

Eva places the box on the table and grins. Dad pulls out a seat for her, as if she's already helpless, so Eva gives him a dig. Seeing it hurts, I give Laura one, just to pass it on. "Laura, Jessica... I'm thrilled to tell you that you are going to have a little brother or sister," she says and he kisses her full on the mouth.

I wish they wouldn't.

It's PRIMEVAL.

But I'm not going to care. We're having a BABY!

Maybe it was just keeping the secret of it that made me feel off.

"You won't have to do a thing. Laura and me'll rotate breakfasts in bed when you get too big to get up. Your legs'll probably swell so you should keep them up as much as possible cos that's what happened Ms Otis. They swelled like balloons but she said everyone gave her seats on busses so it was good too."

"See why I didn't want to say anything yet?" Eva gives

Dad's pigtail a playful tug. "The baby isn't due until September, Jessie."

"You haven't even been sick."

"No. I think this little one is a kind baby! And this little miracle also means quite a change for your father too." Doh! Goes without saying. A baby at his age! He's nearly 40.

Then I see the cake.

"Are they mountains?" says Laura.

As Eva passes Dad two red Smarties, the nasty feeling creeps back in.

"Crematoriums?"

With an encouraging smile from Eva, Dad puts a smartie on top of each mound. I'm guessing that since Eva doesn't do home-made, this cake was ordered at the bakery near the school which means EVERYONE in the neighbourhood knows my stepmother orders boob cakes.

"Dad?" I say.

"Remember what we said to you when we all first talked about us having a baby?" says Eva. Laura shakes her head but the fog in my head is clearing and I want it back. "About how your dad and I had agreed that if we had our own baby to add to the family, your father would be free *to go ahead*."

"Free to go ahead and do what?" says Laura.

Dad takes one of Laura's hands and one of mine and very gravely tells us, "I am going to physically transition into Mandy, the woman I have always known I am, that you have always known I am." He tries not to smile, nervous of how we will respond but joyful, as if he's lit up inside; as if this is the best news possible.

I can't believe I could have been so DUMB but she's right. They had a deal. *Have* had. For years. Only somehow when Eva never did get pregnant – which was sad cos she was always looking at babies – I'd managed to forget because I thought it would never happen.

"Sort of like another miracle?" says Laura. Sometimes I could pinch her.

Dad nods. "For me, yeah."

Eva explains it all again for Laura, as if it were a bedtime story or a fairy tale and maybe it is, for her. How when they met, Dad was Mandy. How she liked women more than she liked men, but fell in love with Dad. How she'd also wanted a baby of her own. But that was years ago.

You can't. Not now. I've made friends. They LIKE me. That's what I want to say. It's what I'm saying in my head only it's so NOISY in there right now, what with all of them looking at me and Dad waiting for my response. As if it all depends on me.

So I don't cry or scream, *You're my dad! Isn't that enough?* I say, "That's great, Dad. Really great." As if we were discussing a new car or whether to go shopping today or tomorrow or in five years time.

Next thing I know, Dad has me n Laura in this big hug. It's arm spaghetti and I can't even smell my own breath or feel my toes so I pull away, apologetically. "Tons of homework."

Dad nods, as if he doesn't trust himself to speak, he's SO relieved and happy and proud of me. Eva starts cutting up the cake and I can't say another word.

Except to Laura, before I leave, "Nuns don't eat cake."

"Oh."

"They fast from cake as a punishment for not having children and they can't," I add, as she heaps sugar into her mint tea, "have sugar either."

"OH but Sister Agnes did."

"And we all know what happened to Sister Agnes, don't we?"

She shakes her head.

"I'll tell you when you're older."

"Cake, Laura?" says Eva.

"No thanks." She's such a goody good. Final score: one-nil to me. A good time to leave. As I close the door behind me, Laura lifts up a bit of congealed meat on her plate.

"Can I give this to the Ponchinello?"

THIRTEEN

To. Go. Ahead.

Three words. Four syllables. The END of life as we know it.

From now on, I will never be able to misbehave in school because if I do, school will call home and ask my parents to come in. I can never have a boyfriend because sooner or later they'll want to meet my dad. Friends? Forget it because eventually they'll expect me to bring them home.

So I knew, once upon a time, that this could happen. That doesn't make it easier. I was little. An ostrich sticks her head in the sand for a very good reason.

It's quiet out on the Cloud Platform; me, Buffy, one soft Tootsie Roll I'm squishing flat so it'll last longer and the sky. I'm glad of Buffy's warmth. Even if clouds could talk, this lot are too far away to be any comfort. I let the Tootsie Roll cover my tongue so I'm not really in a position to talk when Dad appears.

"Better now than in ten years." He sits sideways in the doorway so he can pretend he isn't high up. "When my skin's all old and crabby and I have to hit people with my handbag to convince them I'm a woman."

It's funny, thinking of him like that. Gramma with attitude. But it doesn't matter. Anything that's funny here and now will be funny-strange in a WHOLE different way to everyone else.

Next door, Mr D. drags his compost bin out from the shed in which they hide the bins. Abby says he hates bin day because it makes the road untidy. If he could live in a house that produced no waste, she said, he'd be in heaven.

All I can hear is Buffy purring. I lean back into Dad and close my eyes. It's okay cos Eva has him on something to make him less allergic to cats. "D'you think Mum knew?"

He shakes his head after a while. "But Lizzie was smart, like you. She'd have worked it out." He tucks the hair behind my ears. Normally I don't let him anymore. Makes me feel like a baby. This is the second time this week and I haven't complained. Dunno how he hasn't noticed. "It's not because of Eva."

"I know. I just miss Mum sometimes."

He puts his arm around my shoulders and doesn't say anything for the longest time. As if he's reaching back through the whole of his life and feeling the weight of it; staring so hard into the middle sky that I can't see his face.

"Dad?"

"I miss her too love and I wish I could have told her but that won't bring her back and it won't change the way I feel about this crap body I was given."

"Language!" The joke falls flat. My jokes usually do. It's

not a gene I was blessed with.

"Jessie, we should talk about what this means. It's a very big step for all of us and I can't even predict how difficult this will be, for you especially."

I'm focusing hard as I can on a particular cumulonimbus. *What does he expect from me?* Some of these clouds are 50,000 feet up. We wouldn't even be specks of dust to them.

"You really want this?"

He nods. Except, of course, that now he's saying how glad he was that he could be a man first or Laura and I wouldn't be here. See, he loved Mum to pieces then and didn't know, not *exactly*, what it was that he felt about his body then or he wasn't ready to admit what that feeling meant.

"I want us all to see the consultant together. She knows your opinion is important to me."

So I nod. Again.

I nod because he's sincere and he's my dad and I love him.

Sometimes.

"Come on down and have some cake."

"In a bit."

I stay there with Buffy until the air gets chilly. Then I work on my house for a bit – I have the decor done and I've been working on the furniture – before hunger and concern that all the cake will be gone sends me back downstairs. I've only got to the hall when Dad comes out of the living room with a, "Jessie, great timing. I was just about to call you down."

"I just came down for some cake."

"You can bring it in with you."

Family meetings, group hugs and corndogs are among the worst things we brought back from America. Right now, I'm in a 'what now?' sort of mood. Like when you get a plate of undercooked asparagus but you were *expecting* chocolate cake.

I help myself to a ginormous slice of cake but when I go in, Eva and Laura are already on the sofa. I have a feeling my appetite may be challenged cos Dad looks nervous. Mind you, he's leaning against the tank and piranhas have been known to jump. "All girls together!"

This is cheesier than anything I ever expected Dad to say and pretty ugh but he's grinning, as if he doesn't realise that he has said something really naff. Normally when he fiddles this much with his fingers, I feel the need to shout at him to sit on his hands. Right now, they're kind of mesmerising.

"You know how proud I am of you both, for the way you've accepted who I am and what I'm planning to do. However, I've talked it over with Eva and the consultant and we're all agreed that we want to make sure you don't get left out of the process. I've already mentioned to Jessie upstairs about us all seeing the consultant together. But outside of that, I want you to know that the minute something comes up that you don't understand or you find hard to accept, I promise you we will all sit down and talk it through."

It's not a bad speech. Trouble is, by now, nobody's listening. Something is happening in the fish tank. Where there was one fish, now there are two, three, four.

Laura laughs. "Ponchinello's having babies!"

Dad swivels round, his dress making a swishing sound. "Is that possible?" says Dad.

"Stranger things have happened," says Eva and slips a kiss onto his neck.

Laura looks at me, smug as you like; as if to say, '*told you he wouldn't eat them all*'. I note that there are no ACTUAL goldfish left in the tank. For a golden moment we stand there, feeling – yes, even me – moved by this little miracle. The tank fills up with little golden fish, some with red fins, some with red tails; some, presumably, with teeth.

As we watch, Ponchinello swims over to one of the tiny fish and touches lips. "Maybe they're kissing," says Dad. To prove him wrong, Ponchinello swallows his first 'child'. Sushi. Eva runs into the kitchen and throws up what sounds like an entire month's food for the whole population of Dublin's non-existent sewer-dwelling crocs. (Yet another thing we lost by moving here.)

Bet the baby turns out vegetarian.

"Quick Laura, bowls and a scoop from the kitchen. Jessie, Perspex from my car." Within minutes or, more crudely, the lifespan of three more offspring, Perspex is fitted down the middle of the tank. Ponchinello, who has somehow morphed into a girl, – the irony is not lost on me – is on one side; the littlies are released into the other. They can still see each other but Ponchinello can't – even with her teeth – get through.

"What if the babies start to eat each other?" I suggest, eyeballing my irritating kid sister.

"Let's keep the rest of the Perspex here, just in case," says Dad.

This way, we'll need compartments for each fish. Wonder if they could get confused and try to eat themselves?

We traipse into the kitchen after Eva, Laura talking about how she's created an entirely new species. She wants to call them Golden Ponchi-Lauracus and sell them in school.

I say, "You can't sell them. They're not fish; they're freaks like you".

Eva shouts "ENOUGH! I want that fish OUT of here *right now*!" before she barfs again. Finally, FINALLY, a word of sense. Has she only now realised that Ponchinello is a flesh eater i.e. only one step up from a zombie which at least *once* had a brain or has pregnancy has made her hyper-sensitive so that having a man-eating fish turn into a mother who then eats his – her – young, is too much? Even for her.

"Oh I'm sure you won't be tempted to eat our baby," says Dad, as if it's all some big joke. I think Eva's going to puke again but she grimaces instead.

"Be far too big anyway," he says.

Which I say is disgusting and Laura says is blasphemous. She doesn't know what the word means but feels it's strong enough to protect her little fish AND the baby.

Dad sends me to collect the mugs we used to scoop out the fish as Laura tells Dad that she might sell some of the baby fish in school. "I think I should cos they're unique." Yes, we are safely back on Planet Laura. Normality.

"Maybe I should let Ponchinello play with clown fish next; their babies would look AMAZING!"

While I'm picking up my favourite *The Woman Who Loved Chocolate* mug from the floor, I spot two coloured folders. Instead of leaving them exactly where they are, dork that I am, I pick them up and say, "What are these?"

FOURTEEN

WHEN will I ever learn NOT to ask stuff?

I've barely picked up the folders when Dad's there thanking me and saying how, in all the excitement, he'd clear forgotten the most important part.

There's more?

"I'm just going to wash the mugs," I say. "Any fish from Ponchinello's tank could slime a mug for life, possibly poison a small army, let alone all of us—".

"Mugs," says he, taking them off me, "can wait." If I interrupted him, he'd tell me how rude it was but, apparently, back in Ireland, when you're an adult, anything goes. Double standards? Wahay, come on in and take a seat. Take a gender, any one you choose and throw a party for the neighbours.

"Sit down."

My stomach aches.

"As you know, once we've okayed the process with the consultant, Dr Strauss, the first step on this journey will be for me to live as a woman. No more skulking inside the house, no more hiding behind 'Frank'. I have to live as Mandy outside the home as well as in."

Buffy jumps up on my lap as if she knows I need comforting. This is scarier than anything Ponchinello could do. Even to clown fish. "They insist on this stage because it allows them, and us, to be completely sure that this is a step I really need to take. This is a huge thing for you to take on but it is also a perfect time.

"We're in a new community; nobody really knows me as Frank, which should make it a smoother transition for all of us." He looks like a puppy that has been offered a lifetime's supply of chocolate and is waiting for permission to scoff it all.

"What about your job?" Yep, that's me, blowing a hole in his Happy Armour.

"They hired me for my talent, not my legs. I'm sure they'll understand."

Happy Armour intact with small dent on lower leg only.

"However, as exciting as this is for me, for all of us, it is important that we tell all the people who love us before I tell anyone outside this family, even work. You two first, then Gramma and Gaffa, then friends."

I tune out and cheer up. Dad will never want to tell Gaffa. Therefore, we should get to the summer easy before he goes public as Mandy. Longer, even. If we get till September, well that's a new term. I can tell everyone an aunt has come to live with us cos Dad ran away to the circus. Lion-taming. Great use of his former rugby skills. He can tackle a chair at 20 metres.

By then I'll be fourteen and well settled into being grumpy so I probably won't even have to talk about it much, just grunt from time to time. Nobody will really care cos of all the fuss about the new baby.

"Which is why, Jessie, Laura…"

Okay. I'm listening. He used my name. He's holding the folders out to Laura and me.

"…We do this as we've done everything else; as a family. Go on. Open them!"

My folder is purple. It may no longer be my favourite colour. Inside – surprise, surprise – is a wad of information sheets, leaflets, 'common issues that may arise' stuff printed out from the web, a list of websites. Not only do I have more sheets than Laura but her pages have lots of cartoons and speech bubbles. She'll have halos and moustaches on them all by bedtime.

"We thought you'd want to have some information to look at on your own before we meet the consultant, Dr. Strauss, in case there are questions you want to ask. If there are any you're too embarrassed to ask, put them in one of the envelopes at the back of the folder and leave them for us to respond to in private. Also, when the time comes, you will be equipped with the knowledge to explain, in your own way, what's happening if anyone asks."

"When are we meeting your consultant?" Please say after the summer, next year, undecided…

"We're meeting her on Friday. It was going to be May but she had a cancellation…"

It's official. I hate purple.

"One more thing," says Eva so gently I sit back down. "…You'll find a list of websites in your folder full of useful information but we don't want you looking up any other sites without asking us. Not everyone is positive."

You don't say.

I can't call him Mandy. I never have. He was just Dad in a dress. Besides, my first Barbie doll was called Mandy. If I had a girl dog with floppy hair and big Spaniel eyes, I'd call her Mandy. Up till now, it wasn't necessary to call him anything other than Dad.

"I think we need to consider using the Ding Method," says Eva. And then she smiles.

Clearly Eva is NOT as together as she thinks she is. Even Laura looks to me as if to say, *'Has she lost it?'* We turn blank faces back, devoid of any emotion that might let Eva know that we think she has gone LOOPY.

"It's quite simple. Every time we call your father 'him' instead of 'her', someone goes 'Ding' or 'Bingbat' or some word you choose. We know it is going to be hard to change overnight and we don't want to hurt your father's feelings. But he – BINGBAT – *she* has to be understanding too. We will all make mistakes, no matter how much we support him. *Her.*"

I can't think of a single word that would be big or loud enough but Eva is insistent that we choose. Finally, Laura suggests, "'*Poof*' cos it sounds kind of magical".

Eva says, "Maybe not" and she and Dad grin.

I hate it when they do that on her. Big joke; adults thinking kids are so quaint. So I plough in – and granted, I didn't really think this out first – behind Laura. "I like it. I think it's a perfect word," and I put my arm around her. This makes her grin. (She has a nice grin. A real wide, smily one.) So now we are stuck with it.

Which is worse? Calling your dad *Mandy* or saying 'poof' 20 times a day? Nope. Don't answer that. Won't I be the lucky teen, getting both!?

"My tummy hurts."

Course I wouldn't have said anything if I'd known it wasn't food poisoning or cancer of the bowel but, instead, my first period. Great. Brilliant. It's the most perfect time IN THE WORLD to start haemorrhaging.

As if my body agrees with me: life SUCKS!

~ ~ ~

When I work out what's happening, Eva sends me to bed with an enormous hug, following me up with paracetamol and a hot water bottle for my tummy. She presses her finger to the little heart I added alongside 'BABY' on our calendar. "Thanks Jessie," she says and her eyes catch mine as if she really means it and not just about the baby but about everything. About her and moving house, her embarrassing art, the lack of routine and the fact that nobody knows what there'll be in the cupboard to take to school for lunch.

But mostly because of Dad.

I shrug but she tucks me in anyway. Tight as a sausage roll. She did this the very first time she stayed over, when Dad introduced her to us and said he'd met someone and hoped we'd like her but no pressure. "Do you want me to wait until you are sleepy?"

"You have to work."

"It can wait. What are the long nights for? Besides, tomorrow, since I am going in to see the Gallery, by this stage, my work should be always finished."

"Is it always this yucky?"

"No. Not always. Sometimes they are only annoying. I think, though, if men had periods, there would be three days paid leave and free Jacuzzi visits every month because they could not cope as we do."

Of course Eva told Dad "My little girl is changing into a woman too." Eva thought it would cheer me up to know what Dad said but all I heard was that last word.

TOO.

It's not as if I haven't been waiting for them. In L.A., I pretended they'd been happening, *"Like, for ages; doh!"* and they were sooo boring but today? Of all days?

Buffy curls up on top of the duvet to get the heat that escapes and her weight helps. But first I push my house under the bed. What's the point of building a house you'll never see again when the new one is falling apart?

When Laura comes to bed, she says, "Hope you feel better soon" and kisses me on the forehead as if she were a big grown-up sister, not a pesky little one. It's sweet.

"Nuns can eat sugar now," I say, by way of a gift. "Special Dispensation."

"Will the baby sleep in with us?" Laura says when Dad tucks her in. I'm pretending to be asleep.

He sits on the side of her bed. "She – or he – will be in a cot in our room for the first year. I don't know after that.

Maybe Jessie will move into the attic and you can share with the baby."

Being seven, Laura's easily pleased. She grins enormously and throws her arms around Dad.

Suddenly, I'm not sure I want to give up sharing a room with Laura, though I'll never admit it.

"Pooooo ffff. Poo. Ffff. Poooffff." Laura lies in bed reciting the word, over and over.

"What are you doing?"

"I'm making it into a mantra so I won't forget."

"You don't need a mantra to remember one word." Then, cos I can't resist, "Why did you suggest poof?"

"I was sitting on one." So it's *pouffe*. Not poof. "It's my favourite seat. And it's red."

Figures.

~ ~ ~

I can't sleep but the stairs are too cold to sit on and I'm hungry now the cramps have worn off so I slip down to the kitchen. As I'm making a cup of hot chocolate, I hear them talking quietly in the living room. "See?" says Eva softly. "It was – *is* – no big deal for them. They've always known it was on the cards."

Dad replies, with this catch in his voice, ""My daughters are two very special people." The door's ajar so I see him lean down to talk to Eva's stomach. "And this new little imp – hello Sweetheart! – will be just as special…"

What can she say to that?

She kisses him.

That's the thing with ostriches. There's always a VERY GOOD REASON we stick our heads in the sand. 'Cept sometimes the sand fills your ears and you don't hear the tiger's fangs until they click around your neck.

FIFTEEN

"Right!" Abby leaps in front of me so I have to stop. How can she be so bouncy on a Monday morning? It's not even sunny. "Let me guess. I'm brilliant at this. I know, it feels like someone's dancing on your grave – probably doing a Jedward, but with elephants – and they've been keeping you awake all weekend and now you're properly grumpy?"

"What?"

"No! NO! Now I have it! You're emotionally exhausted cos thoughts of *him* are nibbling, snatching and filling your every waking moment. You are now consumed with a desperate need to be snogged, just once, before you die and the anxiety of it has your nerves all of a frather."

What is Abby on about? She's like a rabbit with fleas. I navigate around her and continue walking. "Boys are rubbish and snogging… Snogging's STUPID and I couldn't be kept awake if I was dead."

"Yeah. But you'd have NO sense of humour either and sure you're just brimming over. Besides, what's to convince me that you're not a vampire? One of the uncool ones who have to go to school and live on a diet of wild pigs."

I give her my WEAKEST smile. "Frather?"

"Cross between flutter and batter and ….something."
She stops right in front of me, all lit up. "It's Jason, isn't it?
You fancy him something awful."

I shrug.

She carries on oblivious. "I knew it. I knew it! You've
been lying awake dreaming about him…"

I don't bother interrupting. Abby wouldn't understand
that there is no point fancying anyone now. I mean, even if
Dad doesn't do anything before the summer, how long will
it be before someone – probably Laura – tells the world
about Dad and his plans to gender jump?

Bethany didn't even get that far. She saw Dad in a dress.
That's all.

Course it wasn't any old dress. She saw him in his lucky
red dress. I don't think she was sure what she'd seen at first.
She might have left and never been sure; Bethany was pretty
good at looking dazed. (It was an expression she practiced in
front of the mirror cos she felt it made her look seriously
mature…)

Only then Dad turned and said, "Hi Bethany. Jessie's
outside watching clouds."

Just like that.

Jessie.

Watching clouds.

Dad in a dress.

Maybe he smiled. He likes to smile. Perhaps he said,
"You know Jessie and her clouds!" Or, "Are you into them

too?" He did NOT say, "Can you help me with this zip" or if he did, it was *before* he turned, when he thought it was me coming in and then, when he saw it *wasn't* me, he apologised and said, very quietly, "Jessie's outside watching clouds".

Bethany told everyone the bit about the zip. The dress became a mini and the legs unshaven as if he was a freak. Which meant I was a freak too. I mean, look at Laura. Saintly Laura and her veil. Eva makes nude statues and uses them for coat stands but she's the 'normal' one.

The school's principal came round. Eva got calls from other mothers saying how sorry they were and, "You know you can divorce him for that?" So much for liberal America! Maybe we just picked the wrong suburb but then Dad's workplace got antsy and suggested he might not be partner material, while one of the firm's partners made a pass at him.

This is why I love clouds. Clouds don't judge you or each other. How can they pass judgement when by the time they have pointed out what form you've taken, chances are you've morphed into something else?

"...You fancy him as if he was the only boy in the WHOLE of creation."

Laura's up ahead with her 'disciples'. She makes friends easily. They wait for her along the route. By the time she turns in the school gate, there are usually six of them. She doesn't worry about what makes them tick or why they are being nice and they like her right back.

"As if he hasn't got acne and BO and only slouches because he's thinking deep thoughts, not cos he's lazy."

Why can't Abby stop chewing on the bone she thinks she

caught? I bet Laura never even thinks about L.A. anymore. Like Dad and Eva, she grows roots sideways and transplants easily.

"You know he's into bugs?" Abby doesn't wait for a reply. "Yup. Wants to be a forensic scientist and specialise in *bugs*. Big bugs. Little bugs. Flesh-eating micro-bugs with rabid appetites. That suggests he's got brains, but means you two are soooo not well matched."

I give her a grimace, so as not to be rude.

"Unless it's opposites, of course. Or maybe it's star signs and you're just fatally attracted to each other by, like, the moon or something?"

"Even if I did fancy him, I wouldn't waste my time worrying about it cos it's NEVER going to happen."

Abby frowns and stops. It takes her a whole 30 seconds to silently process this insanity and catch up again. "So it's not Jason?"

"No."

"And you're not dead n buried– "

"Unfortunately."

She heaves a dramatic sigh. "So how come you didn't hear a word I said until I mentioned his name?" She's right. Of course she's right. "Okay, I'll go first. But if I let you into our family secret, you have to promise you won't tell ANYONE in school."

Great. Another secret.

"Now I'm not saying anything but y'know the book *Jane Eyre*?"

"Saw the film with Dad. Mad woman in the attic."

"Exactly."

"Your father has an ex-wife living in the attic with Alo? Or is Alo the mad wife?"

"No." I can see her mentally tippexing over my sarcasm. "Silly." We're at the school gate and she goes mute. Well, mute as far as her GI-NORMOUS secret goes. "Not a word to anyone," she says. "I'll reveal all later."

~ ~ ~

The day is slow. During a free period, The Exorcist volunteers me and Alice to clean up the hall. How can civic-minded people, organised by Abby's mum, meeting to discuss their *Tidy* Town campaign make such a mess? It's as if an ogre binged on coffee cups and scones and then exploded.

"So, see, he says I'm a natural. For TV. Presenting stuff."

"Your uncle?"

"Yeah. In TV3. Haven't you been listening?!"

I haven't the heart to push for details and this really pisses her off, so that's not bad. Then I mutter something about not watching TV and get a stare that translates as, "You are *WEIRD*" but I couldn't care less.

No, actually, I do care cos I'm sick of people looking at me and thinking they know me when they don't. For one split second between bin bags of waste, or maybe a whole minute, I really want to tip Alice and her smug future career into the bag I've just filled, in the hope that some sweet wrappers stick.

~ ~ ~

Jason is at his locker, sorting through something. There is NO-ONE else around him and he is talking to no-one. Abby bruises me with a manly shoulder hug. "Why don't you just go over and ask him when you two are going on this famous date?"

Doesn't she listen to *anything?* "I told you. There's no point." I busy myself with the mess that is the interior of my locker.

"Course there's a point. AND I know you want to! Look, you were staring over at him with this really intense expression. Don't worry, nobody else was watching! It was as if you were talking to yourself in Spanish or something and it wasn't about frying eggs."

"Eggs?"

"Home Ec. We cooked an Irish breakfast. Such fun. See, now you're too late. He's gone." The bell goes for the end of break. "You've got to take chances when they come! What if he gets knocked over by a bus or eaten by a werewolf on the way home? You'd never know if he really fancied you cos you didn't ask. Seriously, Jessie!"

"I wasn't thinking about him, if you want to know." We head for Religion.

"Right. So you're not merely a cowardly weasel with the most massive crush on one of the hottest boys in the school, you're also emotionally dead?"

"I've already said yes to a date he hasn't asked me on and he hasn't looked at me since so I've blown it and that's probably just as well. Okay?"

"I don't understand you."

"Join the club."

~ ~ ~

By day's end, I've had three run-ins with Alo the Warthog. First off, he made some remark at assembly that I didn't hear but that made everyone look over at me and snigger. During lunchtime, he managed to tip his tray in my direction when he passed, resulting in a soup-spill that missed my lap but seeped into one shoe. Vegetable. Croutons. Could be worse, I thought, mopping out my shoe in the bathroom. He could be MY brother.

End of the day, he tries to hit me with his bag in yard with all his mates watching. I see it coming and duck. His bag misses and lands upside down, regurgitating everything. As I walk off, I catch Jason's eye and he smiles.

He SMILES!

And yes, this makes me soar like a magpie inflated with helium but only until I remember everything else. Still, he *smiled* at me!

~ ~ ~

"Sorry about Alo," Abby says as we walk home. "It's not you, not really. Alo hates everyone right now. I think it's tougher on him having Dad in the same school; as if he has to challenge him or something. While I keep my head low; he sticks his nose up to be shot down."

See? Abby thinks the ABSOLUTE best of everyone.

"He could just be a psycho-bully-thug?" But I don't say it. He's her brother, after all. I haven't told her about the smile. Still processing.

Half way up the hill I spot a cat that looks like Buffy in number 48. Twins, I guess.

"You're not meant to leave me home alone. Burglars could break in and steal me."

"You're not alone. Eva's there. Stick your head into the studio and tell her you're home. Abby and I have to work on this project."

"Dad said…"

"If you're hungry have some crackers n cheese but don't use the sharp knife, use the grater." Abby's mum is at the door, heading out. "Told you a friend would turn up." She pats Abby's head, as if she were a small tame squirrel. "Poor Abigail was so disappointed when we moved here. Nothing but dull adults as far as the eye could see."

~~~

"The car has left the driveway. Repeat: the car has left the driveway."

We have the house to ourselves.

Abby lifts the latch on the last door on the landing. "Don't tell anyone I brought you in here," she says, before leading me into a hot, floral room, with a pile of knitted jumpers on the bed. Within this pile of jumpers is an elderly woman in a pink turban hat who puts her knitting down and beams up at Abby as she fixes her pillows.

"Jessie, meet Moodge, my best ever Gran."

"Hello darling. What lovely long hair you have. Abby love, I'd like a nap now. If you have time?"

Abby spends the next ten minutes making the heads of a

collection of bobble-headed dogs bob. After Moodge nods off, she explains. "'Unless all the heads are nodding, she thinks the world will stop and can't sleep."

"Why the latch on the door?"

She grins. It's a sort of wicked grin that makes me smile too though I don't know what I'm smiling at. "Moodge likes to dance naked in parks when she forgets to take her medication. Generally in a fountain. That's how she got pneumonia three years ago so now she needs to stay warm all the time. She slipped into Dad's last school. Before they found her, she'd taught two fifth-year classes all about the art of seduction."

"Cool."

"Yeah, but they hushed it up."

Mrs D.'s soup is WICKED with so many chunks of veg and potato that I feel almost guilty leaving Laura next door. Alo is home now and we eye each other up but apart from him pretending to flick a spoonful at me, we survive. He seems to abide by some 'no-annoying zone' around his sister.

Once Abby has me to herself again, she starts up again. "Must be something. Mad aunt. Black sheep."

"Honestly. We're normal. REALLY normal."

But Abby's not done with me yet. "An ancestor who slept with Cromwell and liked it? Moodge says every family has some secret. Even dogs have worms and that's why no-one will eat them."

This is when I remember Eva was heading in to scope out the gallery this afternoon, so Laura will be on her own. My Big Sister genes swing reluctantly into action but before

I go, Abby makes me swear to tell no-one about Moodge.

Mr D. doesn't want it getting round the school that his mum is loopy.

~ ~ ~

Laura's waiting with a trowel in her hand and mud on her shoes. "Want me to keep quiet about Dad?"

She's GOOD.

This is how I end up in the back garden digging an enormous rectangular hole for no reason whatsoever while Laura reads aloud from her Book of Saints. She's trying to think of a Saint's name for herself or find a group that is lacking a Patron Saint so she can audition.

"How about Patron Saint of Irritating Kid Sisters?"

I've had enough. She can dig her own hole. Just as I'm downing tools, innocent as you like, she says, "Dad rang."

"When?"

"'S'okay. Told him you were in the bathroom. You've been in the bathroom a *really* long time. I guess I can say you forgot to ring him back cos you were helping me with a *'project'...*" Forty minutes and two broken fingernails later, I leave her tidying up the edges with a scissors. (I said no to her using the shears. I'm not an irresponsible older sister.) It looks like a small grave.

"Who's the victim?"

"No one." Laura jumps down into it and grins. "Just, like, the way you said about saints and all and how they have to die. Thought I'd try out resurrection – since Dad is – before I turn into a saint."

"You're not going to put the soil on top of you?"

"Course not. It'd be smelly."

"Okay so."

After I've washed my hands, I take a wet facecloth and very carefully wipe away the existing chalk line and re-draw it two inches closer to Laura's side.

There.

Now I feel better.

SIXTEEN

Ponchinello has turned red again. She has also stopped swimming upside down. It seems that turning black is a sign of pregnancy in piranhas, while swimming upside down was Ponchinello being odd. Trouble is, since then she hasn't moved. She floats there, staring through the Perspex at the other fish, her mouth permanently ajar.

If she wasn't a fish, I'd swear she was salivating. "She's lonely," says Laura. "Or saying hello."

She is NOT.

It's plain to everyone but Laura that Ponchinello's wondering why her sushi is out of reach and is trying to mind-melt the Perspex out of existence. She probably spends the nights chiselling away with her front molars, trying to find a weakness that will allow her through.

Laura scoops her into a Tupperware container and says I have no soul.

Friday. Everyone LOVES Fridays, right? Last day of the school week; two lazy days, barring homework, to follow? Not only is it a Friday but Laura and I are skipping school.

So far so good?

If we weren't being dragged across town to meet Dad's consultant.

Oh but apparently that's okay cos Ponchinello's coming with us. "She's family too," says Laura, "and a trip out of the tank might cheer her up." Add to this that Dad has decided to wear a cravat. Yeah, I know. Embarrassing. He says it's his lucky scarf but we all know it's a cravat. Even Eva. Least said soonest mended, as the scorpion said to the fox before they drowned.

Finally, to complete the sunny outlook for the day ahead, a City of Zits has erupted across my face. Big ones, little ones and a really ugly skyscraper between my eyes.

Yihoo.

I want this morning OVER WITH.

We arrive early enough for two trips to the restroom (Dad and Laura), two takeaway coffees (Dad and Eva), and a whole set of drawings by Laura in Dad's diary of what he will look like when he transforms into Mandy. I'm calling the zit between my eyes the Taj Mahal and trying to imagine it's a fashion accessory or a Hindi mark.

"You brought everyone. How nice."

Dr Janet Strauss is the least glamorous women I've ever seen. She seems less than happy to see Laura and me and I couldn't agree more. There's a growl right under the surface of her unintentional moustache but she smiles all the same and beckons us in.

"It's important to us," says Dad, "that the girls aren't excluded."

Right now, *excluded* sounds fine to me. I mean, where else could I be? A funfair? Hiding in a cloud? Detention?

"Were you a man too?" says Laura which kind of breaks the ice.

She wasn't.

We go under the ice, submerged and losing the will to live, when Laura adds, "You look like you *were* a man but the operation didn't go too well."

For a beat, all that can be heard is someone singing Happy Birthday down the corridor. Dr Strauss focuses on Dad. "You'll want counselling for the girls?"

"Absolutely," says Eva, possibly to prevent Laura from making things worse.

Laura's having none of it. "I might be a man when I grow up. I haven't decided yet." I give her a sneaky hug. I'm so proud of her sometimes, the way she can say the wrong thing at exactly the right time!

Dr Strauss gives us an ARMY of leaflets and tells us to interrupt if we need anything explained, anything at all. But she's hoping we won't and that's fine by me. I can see she wishes she had a sandpit to drop us into. Laura follows a spider behind the desk and catches it in her two hands. Distracted by how gentle Laura is, Dr Strauss lowers her voice. "Do you know what's going to happen to your father, Laura?"

"He – POOF – *she's* going to be a woman," says Laura. If there could be a shrug in a sentence, it was there. Then she smiles and very, very carefully releases the spider into Ponchinello's container to be swallowed whole.

"Have a doll," says the doctor, when she has recovered from the shock.

"Do saints like dolls?"

"I'm sure they do, love," says Dad.

"Okay."

And so Laura, my adorable sister, gets another doll to dissect. I pity the doll. What they will do to Dad is nothing to what she inflicts on dolls. Neither of us listens much after that, but it's impossible not to catch snatches. I move over to sit in the windowsill and stare out.

"… Once we have decided on your dimensions – I recommend not going for extremes if you want to pass – there's the option to reduce the Adam's apple. Even to remove some jawbone to make the face more feminine…"

Outside, a patient sprouts ENORMOUS breasts; the sort that would put your eye out. By the time I blink, he has disappeared indoors.

"Later on we can look at Botox perhaps for the worry lines, collagen for the lips,?"

A second patient smokes by the fountain but as Dr Strauss speaks, his lips inflate into huge watermelons and topple him into the water. I decide to stop looking out the window but the room's not much better. Graphs and diagrams I barely understand; posters and sample silicone implants in a glass case. It's a torture chamber. Why can't anyone see that?

"For the hips, it is possible to do implants; give you a more womanly shape…"

"But I like his– *her* hips," says Eva, so sharply I turn.

Does anyone in this room *really* need to know this? She smiles, apologetically, at me.

"Jessie?" I go over to Dad and he puts his arm around me. "Lot to absorb, eh?" I nod. Understatement of the YEAR. Fortunately, Dad isn't exactly listening to the thoughts in my head, especially once the consultant starts up again.

"What about the time span," says Eva. "When can we start?"

"Normally, I would say wait six months, a year, but I've checked through all the psychological and physical reports you supplied and if we don't have to wait on grants or loans?"

Eva reaches out to take Dad's hand. Laura climbs onto his lap. Unusual behaviour for a wannabe saint. "We don't."

Course not.

"Then I see no reason to delay."

Dad's face lights up as if he had a glow-worm for a brain. Fantastic.

Eva hugs him. No snogging, which is good. Dad pulls us all into yet another suffocating family crush but I feel numb. Then he's pumping the consultant's hands. His fingers look so pink and his nails badly need a manicure. I realise we have the same hands.

"Small hands." Dr S. smiles. "Nobody will tell from these hands that you were ever a man. My own…" She holds out her own enormous hands. "As your youngest child said, I could have been a man! Now, let's get down to details."

~ ~ ~

"No Botox," says Eva, starting the car.

"Agreed."

"I wouldn't want you looking younger than me."

"Aw Honey, couldn't we have a Botox party?" They're flirting like newlyweds. It's sooo wrong. Especially today.

"No."

"Botox, lingerie… chocolate fondue?"

"*Dark* chocolate?"

"Agreed.

"Okay, but no Botox."

"Cheat."

"Are you gay, Dad?" says Laura as we pull out of the car park.

"Wouldn't be living with Eva if he was gay, would he?"

"Well, technically that happens all the time," says Dad. "People often hide in what is perceived to be normality when they feel threatened…" Oh for Avatar's sake, why can't he just protect our innocence for once!

"But not in our case." Thank you, Eva.

"But when you're a woman, you'll be gay?" Okay, even I don't have the answer to that.

"I guess so, yes." Laura's happy again. Why does she need to ask these things!?

"What are you doing to your new doll, love?" says Eva, finally noticing.

"I'm doing a daddy on it."

WHY does NOBODY else think this is WEIRD?

"When do you want to tell your parents?" says Eva, as if they were discussing moving house or telling them about the baby.

Dad takes the longest time to answer. "Soon," he says at last, meaning *never*.

I feel a twiglet of hope and clutch it tight.

~ ~ ~

We pull off the motorway for an early lunch. Pizza. Garlic bread. Dessert. I can't remember what we talk about, only that Dad laughed easily and at everything. Eva was all kissy and flirty and there was a fantastic set of cumulonimbus right above the building opposite which kept splitting into tiny little moths.

All too soon, we're at the school gate. Laura's out first. We detoured to the house so she could fetch the little fish she's selling to her friends; each in a little plastic bag. I guess their teeth aren't fully formed yet. Ponchinello is alone in her tank again and had started swimming before we left.

I feel as if I've returned from a funeral. Dad is oblivious to any other mood but his own. And yes, I may be a grumpy teenager but I still talk lots. So you would think being mostly silent all morning would be noticed.

"This day fortnight," he says instead, beaming at us, "'*Mandy*' will be dropping her beautiful girls to school…" Then, FINALLY, he looks at me sort of strangely. "You okay?"

What does he expect me to say? The only thing that could have made this morning worse would be if they'd all turned round and said, "*There's something we haven't told you Jess: you're really a boy*". But at least that'd be the end of periods.

"You can take the rest of the day off, if you want. Special dispensation?"

"It's too soon for them to miss school. Routine is important for settling in," says Eva. "Besides, you need to get into work while O'Grady still thinks the sun shines out of your toes."

"It's okay," I say. School bag on one shoulder, I haul my sports bag from the boot onto the other to keep me balanced. "I don't want to miss rugby."

Then they drive off.

~~~

"Not a word. To anyone…"

"Buttttt–" Laura looks disappointed. She can't keep secrets. Has never really seen the point and Dad, well Dad's always been Mandy too. For her.

"We were at the doctor's." I check my pockets for coins. Barely enough. "Shots or tetanus cos we got scratched by a wild rabbit in the garden."

"Nuns don't lie."

"Just for today." I put my hand on her shoulder so she can see I really mean it. And it's not easy, given the weight of my bags. "For me."

"Do we have wild rabbits?"

"I dunno." I walk her down to her school. "Maybe we haven't found them yet?" She senses something in me that makes her nod really seriously. When I hold out my hand, she gives me whatever coins she has and I see her to her classroom door, knowing she doesn't understand what's going on so it's all up to me.

"I hope they're white. I'd like a white rabbit."

And I'd like a hole to follow a white rabbit down. At least there are only four classes to survive until rugby. Then I can be angry and un-conflicted and it's the right way to be; pagan gods help anyone who gets in my way. I hand in my note to the office. It's suitably vague. 'Time off *for a family matter*.' But before I go out to class, I nip into the canteen. As if I were a prisoner in some movie, I feed the coins into the geriatric public phone and dial. I HAVE to get a mobile this year or else.

"Gramma?" I say, calm as a cucumber. (They have to be calm, given they taste of nothing and are mostly water.) "It's Jessie."

SEVENTEEN

There's mud in places I never knew I had. My nails look as if they've been finger painted with the blood of a dying Jabberwock. Rugby was AWESOME.

"So where were you this morning?" says Abby. It's the first chance we've had to talk all day.

"Doctors."

"You sick?"

I shake my head. She seems impressed, as if faking sickness were a mark of coolness. "Alo painted spots on his tongue once. Dad made him drink a whole bottle of cod liver oil. He was humungously sick for 24 hours but Dad said at least his system was cleaned out so he was unlikely to get sick again during term time. Which was right, but only cos Alo decided it wasn't really worth it. Especially since Dad arranged for him to re-sit the maths test he'd missed."

She lowers her voice. "How did you fake it and why? It's not cos of Alo?"

"No."

"So what, you felt like a lie in? I mean, I'd be totally cool with that but I'd never get away with it." That's the thing with Best Friends. They want to know everything. Then they get all excited by the wrong thing or something they've thought up all by themselves. Abby is an expert at this.

"It was a routine visit. Cos we've just moved here, that's all. Not a big plan or a cunning trick. Nothing interesting or covert or clever. We don't do interesting. We're really, REALLY boring."

"Not as boring as us."

"Worse. We put the Bore in Boring."

"No we're not," says Laura. I'd forgotten she was there.

"See!" says Abby.

"Yeah, you can tell we're really interesting by the fact that I have overnight grown a Third Eye. Actually, it's probably my Evil Eye," I point my Taj Mahal in Laura's direction as if it could zap her mute.

"Technically, that's not true," says Abby. "Your third eye helps you see stuff, psychic and all, but it's not evil."

I stop to tie a not-so-loose shoelace so Laura can pass us and move out of earshot. Maybe it's normal in elementary – sorry, *junior* school– to have kids in veils gather disciples but I still find it creepy being surrounded by their butter-wouldn't-melt holy faces. Abby starts quoting statistics about how families who seem the most normal have the weirdest secrets.

"There was a boy in my last school with two mums and they were both witches. Proper Wicca and covens and goat skulls on the wall. He was really cool. I wanted to be his best friend but he said he already had one. It was a one-eyed lion from 17th Century India but I think he was getting mixed up with his spirit guide."

Half way home her Dad's beamer passes. He drives slowly, as if he likes to be seen driving a beamer, which is an Old Man's Car in my book. The back tyre catches a particularly dark and muddy puddle.

The mud, as we watch, rises like a wave and splashes Laura from head to toe.

Thing is, when the watery mud slides off, my kid sister is standing there grinning without a drop on her head or her feet and the mud splatter on her coat is in the shape of a cross. She looks like a Crusader.

"See," she shouts back. "We're not boring at all."

~ ~ ~

Abby hovers, waiting for an invite. And I should ask her in but not today. "I'm sorry but we've visitors coming."

"Have we?" says Laura. I say yes as if it's her fault she forgot.

Abby sort of shrugs as if she's decided to believe me anyway. We stand outside and chat about nothing until it starts to rain again. When I finally make it upstairs loaded with toast, Laura's on the floor of our room handing items out of a cardboard box to Dad who is obediently holding a Barbie doll.

"She's a bit dim," says Laura. "Gramma says if she'd a bust that big she wouldn't be able to stand. This is probably why she needs a horse. 'Sides there's nowhere for her food to go but she probably doesn't eat anyway."

"What are you doing?"

"Teaching Dad to be a girl," says Laura. He grins, sheepish cos he knows it's rubbish but he hasn't the heart to tell her.

"Dad?" I say, "Can we have a bit of space? Girl stuff."

~ ~ ~

"How can he become a woman if he doesn't get to be a girl first?"

Cue Deep Breath Number 537. When dealing with little sisters it is important to have enormous lungs capable of taking very long breaths without causing you to keel over and die. Cos then you'd be dying forever and that would only work if you were a cat like Buffy with nine lives.

Actually, nine lives would not be enough to survive Laura. You'd need a hundred.

Per year.

"You don't understand. They won't be building him from scratch. Well, they *sort of* do, but they don't make him younger first so he won't be growing up into a woman, he'll just be one." Next door, Mr D. installs a Victorian water feature in the middle of their front garden. The word 'why?' comes to mind but it's not my concern.

Deep Breath 538. "They want to cut him up."

Well they do. And someone has to tell her. I'm being the grown-up here and I am fully prepared for the waterworks, the shrieks, the hysteria and the fainting. Even if she lashes out at me or flings things about, I'll hold her tight.

"But they'll put him back together?" says Laura, squinting at me.

"Course they will. Just not the same way. When they're finished, he won't be a 'man' anymore."

"He'll be a woman."

"Yes."

She blinks several times. "That'll save time," she says, cool as you please.

Why is she making this so hard? Doesn't she understand?

"So Dad doesn't need to know about Barbies?"

"No."

"That's good cos they're not very clever. Gramma says their knees are not like real knees at all because they don't bend. Which must be sore. It would be sore, wouldn't it? And Dad doesn't 'do' sore so it can't be 'sore', what Dad's doing. Will we have to watch, cos I don't think I'd want to watch?"

"No," I say. "Because it's not going to happen."

"I think Dad wants it to happen," she says, very slowly and loses interest. "Want to see the book I bought? It's cool."

I give up. I've tried my best. Laura invested the money she made selling Ponchinello's babies in a new Book of Saints, a holy medal and a phial of holy water. "Nope."

I grab a throw then, take my homework (and three Sour Patches as compensation for the frustration of having a sister like Laura) out onto the Cloud Platform. It's peaceful but there's no sign of Buffy and I could do with her now.

Whoever invented homework should be laid on a plinth, covered with hot chilli oil and left in a jungle.

Dad sticks his head out, says he needs my keen eye. Nobody, and especially not teenagers, move quickly when

117

their brains have been pounded with impossible maths equations using the ridiculously vacuous life of Mr Money and Mrs Shop. By the time I climb in and get down to Dad's home office, he's starting back out to call me again.

"Wanted to ask you to look at the plans before I bring them in on Monday." He's in a pale blue cashmere two-piece. It used to be Laura's favourite cos the fabric is soft and perfect for snuggling. "After what you said in the office, I've moved the toilets well away from even the vaguest possibility of smoke to an outside wall and allowed access from both sides for people who are waiting or need some time to reflect before or afterward. That gazebo you suggested…"

Did this morning never happen?

"Also, I was thinking about how things were for you after your mum so I added a playroom, full of toys and books. Somewhere the kids can see the service but make noise if they need. Hard enough dealing with death without them needing to be quiet all the time. There's also a therapeutic meadow of wild flowers, with access from the toilets in case people need to escape for a few minutes."

I put wild flowers on Mum's coffin but I didn't open my eyes at the funeral service cos I wanted to think she could still wake up. Instead, I watched Laura, all cuddled in Dad's arms and wondered how I'd hold onto enough of Mum to pass on to her.

"It's great Dad. I love the copper roof."

He rolls another set of plans on top. The sports stadium. "I have a couple of months more on these, but I thought I'd submit a provisional plan to get a bit ahead, impress the new boss… Any initial thoughts?"

Just then a car pulls into the drive. Puzzled, Dad goes to the window as Gaffa's panther reverses into position with a flick of its tail and a toot of its horn.

EIGHTEEN

"So, how's my favourite twelve year-old granddaughter?" says Gramma, hugging me tightly.

"Fine," I say and I smile. I make it a SERIOUS *Grown-Up Hiding Stuff From Little Children* smile. One that says, I can't talk about it now but you'll understand soon.

"So where's the blushing Mum-to-be?"

"I'll go get her. Laura, make Gramma and Gaffa a cup of tea."

"Forget the tea. I think this occasion calls for a drink," says Gaffa, heading for the drinks cabinet.

Dad fled to Eva's studio when I went down to answer the door so lucky me traipses through the mud that was meant to be a path in a game called *Fetch The Dad*.

Her studio is magical but it's hard not to feel creeped out when you see the outlines and shapes of statues while Salome, she's hanging from the ceiling but now she has glass eyes and looks alive. One word and all these figures would come alive and dance around me until I became one of them, frozen in place, to be gawped at in galleries or hold doors open for the rest of my life.

"They have definitely heard *something*. I know they have!" Dad's pacing up and down.

Eva stands at the centre of his universe waiting for the ebbs to flow and the tide to turn. "It's Friday. They're bored. This is why we came to Dublin. To be accessible to them.

On her back wall, Eva has hung a rainbow of fabric she's going to use for backdrops – deep crimson, sky blue, yellow, gold. On either side, there are shelves of breasts. Some are for a chandelier made out of glass breasts so thin they're almost invisible but most are ceramic. These are for an installation of that she's going to light up from underneath. The *Field of Mammaries*, as Dad calls it.

"The car swept in. It *swept* in!" He stands in front of her, all run out of steam.

"Alright. Maybe you are right."

"What do I do?!"

"You tell them." She takes his hands and rests one of them on her stomach. "As good now as in a week or a month or a year. Whatever happens, this *has* to. The more you delay, the more anxious you will be. It *should* be now. Then you are free to control your own fate." She tidies up his ponytail. "Remember, you are one sexy lady and I love you."

I cough loudly. There's only so much schmaltz you want your parents to know you've overheard. Eva smiles at me to wait where I am.

"I'll go on in with Jessie but we won't say anything till you're there, except about the baby.

~ ~ ~

With a nudge from Gramma, Gaffa hands Eva the cake they've brought, by way of celebrating the "good news". What is it with Ireland and cakes? Chocolates. A nice BIG box of chocolates would be infinitely better. Especially since Dad's watching his weight and Eva is allergic so Laura and I – which actually means I alone – would get them all.

"How did you find out?"

"Oh you know… a little bird said there was some big news!" says Gramma.

"A son this time," says Gaffa, with a wink to me. "Eh? Nothing like a son."

There's a kerfuffle in the kitchen as if teapot is dancing a tango or a giant mouse is making paella. Eva excuses herself. "So long as it's healthy, I really don't care."

Gramma turns to me. "Are you going to tell us what the other big news is?"

No need. Here comes Dad, holding Eva's hand. Tightly. I get the feeling she's holding him up. 'Course Gramma and Gaffa don't even hear them. Gaffa is too busy extolling the virtues of a grandson to his grand*daughters*, which is a bit insensitive; while Gramma sounds a little wistful saying she would have liked a daughter.

A touch ironic now.

"Mum, Dad." Something in Dad's voice makes them turn, slow-mo and then they freeze, staring at Dad. At *Mandy*. He looks quite beautiful when he's made up. If you were short-sighted or you didn't peer too closely, he'd look like an angular but very striking woman but it's always a shock, when I see 'Mandy' through other people's eyes. He smoothes down the skirt with his hands, trying not to fidget or flee.

No-one says a word. Not for ages and ages. Not till it feels as if the sun will set and come up again, only to drop into a bowl of lava and never emerge. Everyone's waiting for Gaffa to speak. Even Ponchinello seems to be holding her breath but Gramma speaks first, being kind and wanting to help Dad – and Gaffa – somehow.

"When your dad was Laura's age, he thought he was a spaceship," she says, to me. "Wouldn't say a word except '*Beep beep. Beep beep*. I'll have that sherry now, Jessie, if you don't mind," she adds… and takes Dad's hand!

I can't believe it! THIS is where his parents explode, make him admit it's a mistake and they'll get him help and what about the kids? Then we defend Dad, only he gives way and everything goes back to being EXACTLY the way it was before. Except that Dad remembers *not* to appear at the door in a dress when I bring friends home.

Gaffa suddenly explodes. "Well, I must say!" He can't seem to stop laughing. Big belly snorts, like a hyena watching Father Ted.

Eva looks at Dad who looks at Gramma who looks at Gaffa. He sees our puzzled faces and erupts all over again. Laura steps defensively in front of her fish tank as if Ponchinello might see her grandfather acting mad while Gramma knocks back her drink and refills her glass.

"You nearly had me there. You nearly did!" Gaffa turns

to me, grinning. "Whose idea was it anyway? Laura? Jessie?" All we manage are short shakes of our heads, which sets him off again. Unable to speak, he points to the date on his phone. "April the First!" Perfect. April Fool's day. "Eva? Frank?"

"Jack," says Gramma, quietly. "Jack, love?"

Gaffa stops.

"Dad, I know it won't be easy for you…" Eva squeezes Dad's hand to encourage him to continue. "…but I'd really appreciate it if you and Mum could start thinking of me as Mandy from now on."

Then he and Eva explain about the years of wanting this, about how long the physical transition will take but that he will start living publicly as Mandy in a fortnight.

He tries to make eye contact with Gaffa but Gaffa won't.

"He wanted to be a train once too," says Gramma, "and a cat of course. Remember that love? Whiskers and all?"

Only Gaffa doesn't respond. Just fiddles with his car keys and looks as if he has swallowed that hyena and it's dancing in his gut.

So Laura starts telling Gramma about Ponchinello. "She's been pining since her littlies went to new homes because she was a father and a mother at the same time and she misses them. And I think she misses swimming upside down and maybe she misses being a boy fish too."

Before she's finished, Gaffa gets his breath back, tugs at Gramma's arm and walks out of the room. She gives Dad an awkward hug and hurries after him.

Why couldn't he tell Dad he was wrong? That's all he

had to do! Dad would listen to his own father, wouldn't he? But then I remember I don't always listen to my dad and the heart bounces out of me and down the street after Gaffa's car.

"At least it's out now." Eva acts as if it all went well. "No more secrets, right Jessie?"

"Sure." I slip out and call into Abby but Mrs D. says she's studying and can't have friends over on a day when she's already had an after-school activity. I say, "My mistake" and head home. It's not that I was actually going to tell her anything. I don't know what I was going to say or what I wanted.

Normality, maybe?

Instead I end up on the Cloud Platform with Buffy and finish my essay on *Democracy and The Family* – yeah, *that* exists; resisting, barely, the urge to write a story about a family eating itself up from the inside. Then I get bogged down in a maths question about two buckets, a bath and a woman called Mary. All I can think of is that Mary will have frozen to death by the time I work it out so I'll have her death on my hands too.

If this platform were 20,000 feet higher, I could touch the clouds. 6,000 feet and I could catch the heavier ones before they became rain. I could RULE nature. Buffy lopes down off the roof and onto my lap.

She fixes baleful eyes on me, massages my tummy and sleeps. I wonder if the cats they mummified in Ancient Egypt were dead first or sleep-drugged. And did it hurt? I mean, did they *know* it would hurt before they drank the poison? Did *they* believe they would be gods in another world?

Next door, Mr D. puts out the trash. If he looked up, he'd see me but he wouldn't see what happened downstairs an hour ago.

I decide the cats didn't know. They were fed honeyed food laced with a gentle sleepy poison that wouldn't make them twist and grimace because that would damage the torso. Wrong reason but the right result. Dad calls out from his office as I'm heading down.

"I wanted to say thanks."

"What for?"

"Oh I know it was you who phoned them." He gives me a hug, all soft and warm. "No one else would have had the nerve! You made me do it and I owe you one." Buffy nuzzles my neck and purrs.

"You have NO idea how hard it is to tell your parents something like this. I mean, growing up here 20 years ago." He pauses as his voice breaks. "Strange thing is, looking back, I think your mum almost knew. What do you think?"

"Dad–"

"Yes, love?"

He's looking at me and smiling, so happy and so relieved that I can't say a word. I chicken out; a great big rooster chicken sort of chickening out. "I'm glad Eva's having a baby.

NINETEEN

Monday morning. Cold n bright. School yard.

Dead centre, surrounded by half the known universe, is Lord High Almighty Bully of the World, Aloysius. This has to be bad. And no, I am not being paranoid. I've been here before, remember? Bethany stood in the centre of the school yard in exactly the same way telling her lies and she was my friend.

There's no way to get to the main door without going through the group but first I send Laura off down to her school. She's my kid sister. Don't have to like her but I do have to protect her. Then I take a deep breath, kid myself that this is just some normal day and I DON'T know they're all talking about me and my family and put one foot in front of the other, feeling the cement, focus on how solid the ground is, no chance of falling through.

Pity.

Everyone stops listening to Alo as I approach, preferring to turn and stare, as if I were a strange mythical beast. If I could sprout horns, I know who I'd be aiming them at. Of course I assume the worst i.e. that Alo has seen Dad in a dress or a skirt out back and I sort of snap, just a little. I'm sick and tired of whispers.

"Whatever he's saying, it's not true."

Time stops. Just like that.

"Dad's having a nervous breakdown," I say. My cheeks burn as if the lie is imprinted there in ketchup.

"Yeah," says Alo, "like who wouldn't with fake boobs everywhere!"

Then I see his camera. This is what everyone has been passing round: pictures of Eva's ceramic breasts. He wasn't talking about Dad at all! At least not *Mandy*-Dad. And he's right. Our garden is full of breasts. "It's her exhibition!"

Abby arrives beside me. She has no idea why I'm grinning, especially as I'm talking to her brother, his crony of misfits and half the school.

"My step-mum's exhibition! About women and sex and control of our bodies and destiny and religion, though not really religion as they teach it here, more pagan really."

I head indoors with the perfect timing of a seasoned comic, bouncing on the cocky courageous balls of my feet as if the day suddenly became everything possible. As if Jason had asked me to go to the coolest gig I haven't yet heard about.

As if Jessie Keane has TOTAL CONTROL over her entire life and everything is all going to work out JUST FINE.

That's when I hear Alo say *one thing more.*

It's not even really directed at me.

"Yeah, but her Mum's still a man."

That means he *sort of* knows. And I go all flat again.

~ ~ ~

Between dissecting frogs, algebra and making Spanish Tortillas – to be eaten by the staff, naturally – I barely have time to talk to anyone. Abby wants to know what's wrong since she knows I called in last night and now she thinks I was going to tell her my secret after all and I can't so I avoid her. Not in a mean way. I just don't want to talk to anyone.

I even get on the road home with Laura earlier than usual but Abby catches up while we're waiting for the lights to change.

"You walk fast sometimes!!!" Laura hangs back when we've crossed over, having spotted a disciple behind us and Abby leaps in. "Don't – please stop – I can't bear it – don't tell me! You have, like, a ginormous secret and it's driving you insane." I keep on walking. "Maybe *you're* the secret weirdo! Admit it, you SMILED at my brother, which proves my point. You're not well!"

"Abby, please."

"You do know that if you could share this secret that's making you insane, you'd feel human, right? I mean, seriously; you'd feel *seriously* better."

"Just leave it."

"Torture me with swizzle sticks!" She clutches my school bag as if it were a life saver. "Make me do seven times tables or dance the *Merengue* or kiss Jimmy in 1F who's collecting foul smells...but don't – DON'T tell me!"

It's not far. I don't have to tell her anything.

She falls into place beside me with a great slumping of shoulders, all fake disinterest as Laura tags on with her friends. We're half way up the hill when she turns on her greatest weapon – these big pleading, dying-of-a-plague-and-you-have-the-cure eyes. Despite myself, I laugh. I can't help it; she's funny.

"That's good," she says, "at least it's not me."

"It's not."

"Did Jason diss you? Are you moving again? Your dad's taking you out of school to send you down the mines, which is what I'd do with you?"

Ha ha.

"Oh come on, Jessie," she says, carving faces into leaves pulled from hedges. "How bad can it be?" She scatters her creatures high into the wind and one of them lands on Laura's makeshift halo. Didn't I mention the halo? That shows how mussed up I've been. It was 'created' at the weekend. Doesn't even bother me. Much. I can pretend it's a hair-band.

"Eva is clearly NOT a man, despite what my idiot brother said yet you've been quiet as a mouse all day since. In PE you threw the basketball so viciously you knocked him into the wall and you didn't even smile!"

Ten yards to go, Laura overtakes and throws Abby's leaf-carving into my face.

"I told you everything," says Abby. We're at my house when she realises I'm not about to tell her anything. "I thought we were friends."

I see RED.

"So your Gran's batty! She's not even proper mad and your parents keep her hidden anyway so it's not as if anyone ever has to know!" The last bit's sort of shouted cos she's running right across her Dad's neat lawn, not through the archway or anything, so I know I've hurt her really badly.

"Abby!" I shout but she doesn't look back. "I didn't mean— "

And then, cos Laura's there by the front door with her angelic little eyes, I stomp inside as if nothing happened.

"Is her Gran really batty? Should I pray for her?"

~ ~ ~

So I can't be friends with Abby. I'll survive. I've done it before. Besides, I have my sister, I have Eva, I have my wonderful, mad Dad and there's a whole new baby coming. I won't even have time for friends.

"Hey," says Dad, handing me a carrot stick when I abandon homework and go in search of company. "Delivered the crematorium today and prelims for the stadium."

"Great." I act as if nothing has happened. What's changed really? We're in Ireland, that's all. It's not as if I know Abby as well as I knew Bethany. This is damage limitation; it's not personal. "Dad, about the coaching, we could go to the park now? Show me some new throws or correct my technique or teach me some tactics—"

It's all for nothing.

"Not exactly dressed for it, love." Yeah, right. It's a great big joke. He's right. Of course he's right. I'm an IDIOT.

He's wearing a floral dress that could best be described as NOT A GOOD LOOK. But get this, he doesn't even turn. He doesn't turn and see that right now, right at this moment, I NEED him to do *something* with me that makes me feel normal. Even if it's only a crummy hug. But of course that's not important. He's going to be a woman after all. Must have fried his brains already.

He doesn't even notice when I leave the room.

Eva follows me out. "Give her time," she says. "She's got a lot on her mind."

I slam the bedroom door behind me. "HIS mind," I mutter. "It's still HIS mind. He hasn't changed yet."

"Will they take his mind apart too and make it a woman's?" says a little voice behind me.

Laura.

How does my freaky little sister hear everything? Her hands are covered in newsprint and glue. She's making a gravestone out of papier maché.

"Yeah," I snap. "They're going to remove his brain, pickle it in vinegar and feed it back to him with a straw." I grab the first item off the shelf that will get me into Abby's house. "Your halo's stupid."

~ ~ ~

Before I can ring, the door opens. Mrs D. is on her way out. By the time Abby comes down, slowly, her Mum is the proud owner of a black-and-white cow with a nodding head – *Welcome to Nebraska* – and a confused expression.

"Why… it's lovely, dear. Isn't it, Abby?"

"She's lending it to me for a project." Abby takes the cow and me upstairs as the door closes behind her Mum. We go straight into Moodge's room. Before I lose my nerve, I move around the room nodding dogs' heads and tell her about Dad dressing as a woman and that Eva's being pregnant means he's going to become a woman for real...

And she doesn't bat an eyelid.

Behind us, Moodge knits a fluorescent lime-green polo-neck, with GEORGE – Abby's dad, Mr D. – written across the neck like a noose.

"You should have told me," says Abby, but not in an angry way or the disappointed tone parents use to make you feel bad. And then it all floods out.

"It's just... He's always dressed as a woman. That's normal. For us and him. It's who he is and I thought that was enough. But every time someone finds out, it goes all weird and screwed up and he never gets how it affects us, like in school and stuff. He misses it all because we all protect him from it."

We sit there silently untangling some coloured wool for Moodge. "Could be worse," she says, finally.

"How!?"

Abby grins. "At least Eva isn't becoming a man." Now I'm grinning too. It's a really daft idea. "Now *that'd* be DISGUSTING."

This is when I know we'll be best friends FOREVER. "Promise you won't tell?"

She nods. "We love secrets, don't we Moodge?"

Moodge smiles at her sweetly. "Is it time for tea, love? I wouldn't mind some tea."

"I'll go get you some," says Abby.

"And maybe a few chocolate digestives. The ones your father likes."

"Wait here," Abby says to me. "I'll be back with a feast!" She pokes her head back around the door. "D'you know what will be the weirdest thing?"

"What?"

"Hugging him, when he has breasts."

And she's gone. It's a thought. It's definitely a thought.

"What was your dad like, Moodge?" I'm not expecting an answer until it comes.

"Hard man. Very misunderstood," she says, quietly. A car pulls up outside our house and a baldy-headed crow of a man steps out. "Soft, yes, soft eyes at the end. Like a moocow. A hairy moocow."

Why is Dad's boss coming to the house AND in the evening?

"Sorry," I shout into the kitchen to Abby as I dive out the door, "I have to go!"

TWENTY

As soon as I enter the house, I can hear Dad's voice soon but I could smell O'Grady's aftershave from the driveway. "So from the air, the stadium will resemble two half footballs."

O'Grady stands beside Dad, his moustache bristling with self-importance, looking down at the plans on the table. They have their backs to the door and don't hear me come in. Dad's dress has disappeared under a pair of jeans and a jumper but it looks as if he is hiding a small squishy alien underneath. He's pointing out the features of the sports stadium.

"Reception centre and exhibition hall here, sports arena, bars, conference facilities. All very rough as yet but you can get the overall idea."

I can hear the excitement in his voice. "See these panels?" He LOVES explaining his ideas. "The glass in them can be adjusted to capture the maximum amount of light and direct it into the building."

I'm leaving them to it when O'Grady speaks. "Two breasts."

Okay. I wasn't expecting that. Dad cocks his head to one side, the way he does when he wants to agree with you but doesn't know how. "No, footballs. Definitely footballs."

"So what are these?"

"Aerial platforms. We discussed this. You wanted to create tourism opportunities. Lifts will effectively transport visitors into the sky above the stadium. Panoramic views and up top, in the platform, anything you want: restaurant, museum, bar, shop…"

O'Grady licks his lips and shifts his feet. "Nipples."

"Really?"

O'Grady rolls out another next set of plans. "And this?"

"That's the crematorium." Dad's not sure where this is going, so he plays for time. "I'm guessing you think it resembles–"

"Another breast." O'Grady places a bag on the table and pulls out Dad's navy heels. "Found them in your drawer when I was looking for a sharpener."

"Looking for a sharpener. In *my* desk?"

"Tell me they belong to your wife."

Dad doesn't say anything until he catches me watching from the doorway. "No," he says, very clearly. "They're mine."

O'Grady rolls up the plans and hands them to Dad as if they had been dragged through dog poo on the way in. "I'm sorry. I really am." (He's not.) "But we're a respectable family firm with a long and distinguished history."

"I moved my family from America for this job!"

"On a contract basis, as you insisted."

"You can't sack him."

"I'm not 'sacking' your father, Sweetie."

"Yes you are and it's discrimination. Dad's a brilliant architect and you know it."

"Come on, Jessie. Not that bad. More time to spend with you and Laura."

"Dad, designing is your life and these plans are awesome."

"I'll go freelance. I'm sure there are plenty of less narrow-minded firms out there."

"While you work that out," says the baldy coot, "here's a copy of the contract. I've highlighted the official backing 'out' clause which O'Grady & Son is now enacting." By the time Dad has taken the contract, the skunk is halfway to the front door. The door clicks shut behind him as if it's relieved.

"Come here you!" Dad pulls me into an embrace and everything suddenly feels okay.

Eva comes in with a takeaway. "What did he want?"

"Oh, to sack me. But you should have seen our little Squirrel. Took him on as if she were a born-again Baptist."

Then I know it's not okay. Nothing ever is.

"Let's eat before the food gets cold."

Yup. That'll fix everything. She always says this. Even if it's a salad.

"Jessie?"

"Nothing."

"You okay?"

What can I say? "Ravenous. Unbelievably ravenous. I could eat a skunk!"

~ ~ ~

"I was talking with Jennifer, your friend's Mum today," says Eva.

Dad steals the last chicken ball. He's always so FAST. Dad's carrots are still in cold water on the stove. "Didn't think you had much in common with her."

"When you get to know her, she's really quite sweet–"

"Which means?" says Dad to me, as if it were an oral exam.

"Eva doesn't like Abby's Dad," I reply, right on cue. Laura disappears into the living room with a lump of sweet n sour chicken for her precious fish.

"He's an oaf."

"I can't understand how an intelligent woman can put up with such a man. Masticates each morsel 15 to 25 times to trick his digestive system into keeping him thin."

"Must be like having dinner with a gerbil!" says Dad.

"It also means that dinner has to be on the table at 6.35 exactly so he can have a brandy watching the six o'clock news in peace and quiet."

"They take an interest in their kids," I mutter. Might as well be invisible. At least then I could toss Ponchinello into the blender. "At least they check their homework and do packed lunches and make them eat broccoli." Okay, so I'm not exactly thinking with the brains I'm reputed to have but sometimes it's hard to find the words when everyone else says sounds so stupid and unfair.

"You hate broccoli," says Eva, surprised.

She's right. Of course she is.

"We all hate broccoli," says Dad. It's there, sitting in the congealing sauce.

"That's not the POINT!" Now I have their attention. "Abby's mum cooks proper dinners and irons their uniforms and gives them hot chocolate before they go to bed, to help them sleep!"

"You want me to iron your uniform, like some housemaid?"

"Course not!" She just doesn't GET it. "I was just saying…" Why isn't anyone talking about why Dad got sacked?

"Ponchinello–" Everyone turns. Laura's standing very quietly in the doorway, her halo in her hands. "Ponchinello's dead." Which at least stops the conversation going around in any more circles, NONE of which I can ever win.

Ponchinello is floating on top of the water, as dead fish do, but nobody reaches in to lift her out. It's as if we can hear her little evil fishy mind thinking, *"Wait for it, wait for it…Wait for it…"* I know she'd take our fingers off. Even dead, she'd try.

"Can I get another piranha to eat her?"

"We've got a cat for that, love," says Eva.

"You're not feeding Buffy your poxy fish." Eva turns to Dad for help. It's not fair really. She does her best but sometimes we're hard work.

"Let's bury her in the garden," says Dad, fishing Ponchinello out with the pasta scoop. I'm never using it again.

"Proper grave?"

"Sure."

"Headstone? Prayer Service? Flowers?"

139

"Love, she's only a fish."

"Fish have souls."

I leave them to it. Can't even feel happy the beast is dead. Or bring myself to tell Laura it's her fault since Ponchinello most likely died of frustration after watching all that live bait swimming up and down, out of reach, day after day.

"What if she resurrects herself? Like a saint fish?" I groan – nobody hears – but her next question stops me at the door. "If you haven't got a job, will we have to go back to America?"

~ ~ ~

"Maybe this was a bad idea," says Dad.

Finally, says I, in my head. They're washing up and talking really quietly cos Laura's in the other room praying over Ponchinello so he'll get reincarnated. Probably as a Pit-bull. I was bringing all my mugs back down but now I stay outside the door, listening instead.

"Maybe Ireland isn't ready…"

"O'Grady is one man with a dirty mind," says Eva. "He is not representative." So it's only the job he thinks is a bad idea, not his transformation. "Besides," I can hear her smiling, "I think it would be wonderful to be cremated in a breast!"

Can I have new parents PLEASE?

"Maybe it is all too fast. I'll ring Dr Strauss in the morning, ask her about postponing everything until I get another job."

It dawns on me then. Everything is going to be alright. I could be missing something but right now, I could hug boomy Mr O'Grady. Especially as I know it'd scare him. I'd hug him and tell him that Dad only ever draws boobs and what's more, he only ever wants to draw boobs.

I leave the mugs in the hall and go upstairs. Laura's already asleep but I feel fidgety so I work on the kitchen furniture until my eyes get tired. Then I sleep like a baby piglet in a swamp of melted butter.

TWENTY ONE

Abby stares sideways at me, suspicious. "You're looking happy. You never look happy in the morning. Granted, you might resemble a spewed up toad or a slightly-less-miserable squished cabbage, but happy? NEVER! And where did you run off to anyway?"

"We had a visitor."

"You do realise you totally blew our cover story with Mum, about working on a project together?"

"What did you say to her?"

"Nothing. Absolutely nothing. Trouble is, usually I tell her all sorts so now she thinks this is serious and says I'm not to speak to you until you apologise. Besides you left Moodge's door open. She cornered Dad in the garden before tea and forced him into that jumper."

"Is she okay?"

Abby frowns, then breaks into the widest grin and grabs my arm. "She's been smiling ever since. Dad's been a grump. Everyone who hiccups during assembly today will get detention." She says he already disapproves of chocolate, smiling without cause and apple crumble.

I'm too in love with the universe right now for this to bother me. So, when she lets me get a word in, I tell her about O'Grady's visit and his limp handshake and that Dad's plans make him nervous. I tell her about the job.

"But that's awful," she says.

"He'll get another. I mean, I'm sorry n all but his designs are wonderful so he'll get work. Eva has a handful of commissions already lined up for after her show. This is a good thing."

"I don't understand. It's grossly unfair – and sexist. Why aren't you upset for him?"

"No job – no money; no money – no surgery; no surgery – no point Dad coming out as Mandy. See?"

Abby doesn't say anything for a while. The words, when they come, seem almost reluctant. "Laura's not going to get to be a saint until she's dead," she says. "Doesn't stop her dressing as one."

~ ~ ~

Gaffa is waiting at the gate after school. "Thought I'd like to spend some time with my grandchildren." He looks out of place but hugs soon have him beaming again. "How about we go for an icecream?"

It's not the time to talk about homework. "We'll still love you when Dad's a woman," says Laura when we reach his car. I could have kicked her only then she'd squeal and he'd know. It's not that I want Gaffa to feel bad but he has to *need* to stop Dad and that makes me mean.

This whole thing makes me mean and I don't like myself. Gaffa looks frail and I've never noticed him looking frail before. All the bluff and bluster is gone.

Besides, what if Abby's right? What's to stop Dad living as a woman anyway when he's come this far? Maybe it's too late for him to stop?

~ ~ ~

"Couldn't you just talk to him?"

We've re-convened in Moodge's room; the one place Alo will never enter. We made a big show of making up, with hugs and Mrs D. dumped her healthy eating plan and gave us iced buns with which to secure the reconciliation before she slipped out to deliver fliers. All her committees and worthwhile deeds keep her busy.

Moodge is restful to be with. You talk or you don't. Abby and I, sometimes we sit against the radiator and say nothing at all.

"Because he'd know I lied in the first place."

"But he'd understand why."

~ ~ ~

Thing is, Abby was right. Dad's firing ahead with his 'transition'. Money – "Aren't we lucky?" says Eva – is not an issue. That's what's great about having a commercially successful artist as your partner, Dad says, whose work always sells for huge sums of money. We could have had swanky holidays and a foreign *au pair* who taught us twelve languages before I was ten only Eva invested her money 'wisely' and so money is not an issue, even with Dad out of work.

Temporarily of course.

~~~

"Thought you got on really well with your dad."

"We do… but we've never done *this* before. We've never dealt with something so BIG or that means so much."

"What about your mum? That was bigger than this."

Yeah. It was. I was younger than Laura then and it felt as if the world had ended but that was then. This is now. "We used to talk about her but not for the longest time. If he knew I wanted to stop him doing this, he'd be really hurt but if he works out for himself that it's a mistake, then no-one's to blame and he'll be fine."

"Who's there?" Moodge wakes up all befuddled.

Abby sits up on the bed and hugs her. "It's me, Moodge. Abby, and my friend Jessie from next door."

Moodge takes Abby's hand and mine and holds them a moment before letting go and picking up her knitting as if she had never been asleep. "Not much fun being a woman, girls but you'll be so much better at it than I was. But whatever you, Abigail love, don't be a Cinderella. She got locked into a tower and fed pet food."

"Wasn't that Rapunzel, Moodge?"

"But that's IT!" I give the old lady my bestest hug, but awkwardly, to avoid her knitting needles. "You're a genius, Moodge. I mean, Mrs Darcy."

And though she clearly hasn't a clue WHAT I'm talking

about, she hugs me right back. Her cardigan is soft, exactly how I'd imagine the inside of a cloud to feel. "You're very welcome, dear."

Abby follows me downstairs. "What did she say?"

"*Not much fun…*" She doesn't get it. "*Being a woman.*"

"Oh right!" Then she shakes her head. "No. I still don't get it. What has that got to do with your dad?"

~ ~ ~

Abby's mum is back, dredging clothes out of the washing machine when we land in the kitchen. "Mrs Darcy, what's the worst thing about being a woman?" She doesn't even hesitate. Maybe it's because housework is boring and repetitive. Or maybe it's the once-was-white shirt glowing pink in her hands.

"Tights. Ladders in your tights. Make up. Never liked it. Being under pressure to keep everything running so smoothly while nobody – not one! – appreciates all the work that goes into it. The housework, the routine, the endless goodwill! Having always to be nice. To smile. To pretend interest in everyone's news–"

Wow! Step forward the REAL Mrs D.! I think she realises she's said too much and pulls back with a, "But you don't want to hear about that!"

Before she can stop us, I have the front door open and drag Abby out. "Abby's coming to tea, Mrs Darcy. Byeeeee."

"Here!" I hand Abby a wad of discarded women's mags from the paper bin. Eva likes to keep track of their content to make sure her work is informed. Sometimes she does montages too, within backdrops to installations. The *Field of Mammaries*, for example, will have one about society's misrepresentation of the female form. I grab a pile of newspapers, freesheets and supplements. "We can get the rest later."

"Jessie?"

"Come on." I don't say a word till we're safely in the bedroom, our loot spread across the floor. "I saw something here–" There it is. A two-page article: *My Breast Implants Exploded at 30,000 Feet*! "See!"

"Not *really*." says Abby, VERY carefully.

"Think about it." I hand her some scissors. "There's no way Dad will want to be a woman if he knows how awful it can be!! We cut out anything that makes being a woman sound painful, uncomfortable or plain embarrassing–"

"Like this?" She holds up another article. 'Big Toe Exploded After Thug Bounced On My Stilettos'.

"Absolutely!" I make space for three piles. "Physical problems this side, psychological ones on the bed. Anything else goes here."

It's amazing how many odd stories there are. I'm not sure if I should be disgusted or pleased but for the purpose in hand, the worse the better. It feels so good to FINALLY be doing something. The fact that my latest nose zit is larger than any I've had before, that Jason flirted with Alice right in front of me in yard this very lunchtime, none of it seems important anymore. Though I suspect the zit will be important again tomorrow when it explodes.

"Did you see Mum's face?" says Abby.

"Not as bad as this," I say, showing her a photo of a face lift-gone-bad. We both shiver.

By the time Laura waltzes in, we have 15 usable pieces. She's made herself a black armband. "Ponchinello died," she tells Abby.

"Oh, I'm sorry," says Abby. "Who's Ponchinello?"

See? I don't always give out about Laura. Sometimes I can ignore her for days and forget she exists. If I can make Dad change his mind, I promise to never ignore her completely ever again.

Or at least rarely, since I'm pretty sure of winning this one now.

TWENTY TWO

"From now on we ask EVERY woman we meet what's the WORST thing about being female." I pass Abby a note book marked SURVEY in big green letters. This is a military operation.

"Why?" says Laura. I thought she was miles behind with her little acolytes. She catches on pretty quick sometimes.

"Just because."

"And if anyone asks?" says Abby.

"Research. School project."

"Can I have a notebook too?" says Laura.

"When you stop wanting to be a saint."

~ ~ ~

School Nurse McCarthy is gentle and motherly and the boys love her. "A project," I say. "About women's health." She doesn't budge. "Ms O'Flaherty says there's a talk coming up." (What talk? There's ALWAYS a talk. We're at that age. It'll be about boys – again – or drugs or how spending hours on the computer will turn us into zombies with enormous uni-brows but it's a reasonable bet there WILL be a talk.)

"She said we should do some research, so we know what questions to ask and I thought, who better to ask?"

Flattery always works with adults; nearly as good as hugs but I am NOT hugging Nurse McCarthy. I'd suffocate. I can imagine boys wouldn't have the same concern.

"It's wonderful," she begins, ushering me into her office, "…being a woman." This is NOT what I want to hear, though I'm kind of glad too, but it's only the official line. After a few minutes, we hit the jackpot. "Provided you don't let men take advantage of you. Cos they will. They will WALK all over you and bleed you dry and if you have a kind nature… you won't even see it coming."

She's shredding post-its and rolling the pieces into tiny beetles.

"Sure they'll smother their words in honey and make all sorts of wild and glorious, earth-shattering, mouth-watering promises. Not just the men…Oh no! Women are even worse to their own–"

Then, just like Mrs D., Nurse McCarthy remembers she's talking to Jessie Keane from Second Year and skids to a halt with a flick of an eyebrow. Handing me a pile of leaflets, she opens the door for me to leave. "You'll be fine," she says. "Let me know if you need anything else."

'Drawback of becoming a woman = LUNACY', I write on page one of my notebook before transcribing every word she said.

Abby has more luck with the dinner lady. "Large breasts mean back ache," she reads out. "High heels can damage your feet and ankles for life, unless you get stabbed by them. I added that bit cos I'm sure I heard something once... Women age worse than men. Female actors get fewer decent roles or get cast as the mothers of men their own age and criticised for having toy-boys."

"What's a toy-boy?" says Laura.

"An action man for grown-ups." I wish she wouldn't creep up on me. "What are you doing up here?"

"I forgot my lunch." I give her mine. It's only a slice of pizza sandwich and an apple but I've lost my appetite anyway. I dive off to intercept Sr. Maria, the only visible nun in St Brigit's, soon as Laura heads off. Nuns choose not to have anything to do with men so they must know something we don't, but all I get is some stuff about female martyrdom, sacrifice, offering it all up, and "waiting for marriage".

This is NOT exactly useful or illuminating on the Dad front.

I return to the table, totally DESPONDENT. No sooner have I sat down than, "Jessie Keane to the Principal's office immediately" comes over the tannoy. This CAN'T be good.

"I think that's you," says Abby.

What have I done now?

Maybe the Warthog has been telling tales to Daddy, in which case I am MORE than ready to retaliate and would enjoy a battle, really. Right now, I am SPOILING for some sort of fight I stand half a chance of winning. I go into Mr Darcy's office all fired up, tie straight, the lot... and end up standing for an ETERNITY while he finishes signing something.

Waiting is HARD.

Especially when there's a huge plate of chocolate digestives on his desk calling to me individually by name and saying, *you gave away your lunch; you must be starving. Ah go on, have one of us. Maybe two. He'll never notice.* By the time Mr D. gestures me to a seat in front of his desk, I am totally DEFLATED *and* RAVENOUS.

It's not a strong position.

He moves over to look out the window, as if there's something riveting to see when it's only kids in grotty uniforms. Then he starts this rambling speech about women that is TOTALLY inappropriate and all about my "beautiful aunt".

"She *is* an aunt, Jessie? This lady... or is she another Mum?"

He nibbles around the edge of a digestive and that's when it dawns on me: Mr D., he FANCIES Mandy! I'm on my feet before I even think about standing up, making excuses about being late for class, second warning. "Promised I'd help chop up centipedes." *Why would we chop up centipedes?* Fortunately, he isn't even listening.

"I want to understand."

I back away slowly, one step at a time, no sudden moves...

"Maybe an introduction?"

Is every adult mad? "I'm not sure your wife would appreciate that," I say, but only in my head. It's getting pretty crowded in there, what with secrets and plans and trying not to even think about Jason and his beautiful eyes.

Soon as I'm out, I run like, well, a very fast runner and stop millimetres short of crashing into Ms O'Flaherty. Again.

"Being a woman?" I say, whipping out my notebook. I need to sort this out *fast*.

"So *now* you want to know." She caught me doodling in class when she tried to give us the last 'talk'. It's one of her 'roles' as our form tutor aka moral guardian and religion teacher.

"Yes. I want to know. What is the WORST thing about being a woman?"

"Apart from the obvious?"

"Oh, including the obvious," I say, smiling. "I'm really interested."

"What's wrong with you?" says Abby, when I slide into the seat beside her in class.

"I never want to be a woman," I say.

TWENTY THREE

The Survey is done. A week's labour of love, grim but effective. I've called it: *Womanhood, The Agony of Being*. I open with a summary of the relevant categories:

1. Health issues

(Picture: *The Scream* by Munch)

Periods. Enough said. They last for up to 40 years. Leaflets enclosed. Periods cause backache, cramps, headaches, migraines, muscle pain, tiredness, growliness, discomfort, excessive need to eat pasta and chocolate leading to muffin belly and spots, weariness, lack of energy and "nobody understands". Ever.

Migraines: pain, loss of earnings, the need to be alone in a dark room seeing nothing. Possibly caused by on period pain or being on the Pill for too long.

Pre-Menstrual Tension (PMT). Similar to road rage only bigger, more irrational and not confined to car. Can last weeks. Will make you impossible to live with and aggressive. Women can kill under the influence and get away with it.

(Note to self: *scrap last. Too positive.*)

Also, STs and tampons are subject to a luxury tax. I mean, *really!?*

2. Body

(Pictures: spinal traction machine, widow's hump, seriously bandaged torsos after dodgy implants.)

Back pain from overlarge breasts. Implants explode, leak, make sleeping on your side impossible which leads to snoring, loneliness, potential depression. This results in more cosmetic surgery, bankruptcy, marriage to elderly millionaire playboy with dodgy hip. In turn, this may lead to murder charge and jail and all the bad things that happen in a women's jail.

Being judged by appearance. (See (3)), pressure to diet in order to gain or maintain 'perfect' (unnatural) shape. Bulimia. Anorexia. Developing a hyper-critical inner voice re all body parts. Shaving under-arms, legs and bikini wax. (*Whatever that is, it can't be good.*)

3. Appearance

(Pictures: Botox face gone wrong. Bad fashion pics. Close up of cuts on hips caused by wearing 10lb Gypsy Wedding dress).

Impractical clothes. Expensive. Underwire bras give flesh wounds when the wire gets free and cuts in. Men stare at you for reasons other than your intelligence. Becoming a slave to beauty. The cost of make-up, lotions and eyelash tattoos. Shaving/Waxing. Regularly. Plucking eyebrows.

Never being judged for the person you actually are. Worse, you might start to enjoy being judged by your looks or start judging yourself which leads to personality defects such as 'poodle posing' i.e. extreme vanity, stopping frequently to look at yourself in car mirrors and windows and poor decision-making that can result in choosing old husbands, dancing topless at public events – or in fountains – and singing for no reason in a Jacuzzi, even when it's empty.

Removal of facial lines by Botox. It's a poison that freezes the muscles and costs a fortune; how can that be good? Or worse, face lift that leads to permanent disfigurement and a look of shock that you can never lose.

Medical issues: Anorexia. Bulimia. Muffin bellies.

4. Feet

(Pictures of deformed toes, including Chinese bindings.)

High heels cause: Sore toes. Bunions. Dropped arch. Ingrown toenails. Tripping. Head injury. Bad hips. Broken ankles. Feet damaged for life.

Botox in feet to survive the six-inch heels necessary to wear for the Oscars and other big events.

5. Legs

Tights ladder. Underpant elastic doesn't last. Stockings pinch and are draughty. Ugly underwear called 'spanks' cost a fortune. Need to wear high heels to show off legs and stop saggy bum. (See (4)).

6. Treatment by men

Never talking back. Never being heard. The need to be always nice. To be a Maltese mother. (This means putting everyone else first.) But do they respect you? For example, is there a negative male version of slut? There is not. Most of housework and child rearing still done by women because it is not valued. And nobody ever notices.

7. Keeping fit.

Pressure to spend hours in the gym, which is BORING and will speed up dementia out of boredom. Unless you have a heart attack first. Danger of starting to find 'six packs' attractive. Temptation to take steroids and start lifting cars into the air for no reason.

Odd diets that include fasting, watching calories constantly, eating weird foods that taste horrible.

8. Manners

Better manners are expected of women. From listening politely to bores through to salving men's egos and pretending we are not better than they are. Ooops, scratch that. Note to self: remove everything that could be interpreted as POSITIVE.

9. Breasts

Too big, too small. Attract too much attention or not enough. Will get in the way and eventually flop. If too big, or too floppy, they may be sore to carry and bad for your back. Nipple piercing may lead to madness, fear of magnets and dementia. Fake breasts explode in aeroplanes. (See (2) above) Grief. And the risk of breast cancer.

10. Ageing:

Saggy breasts and chicken wing upper arms. Hairy chins, moustache and pain of plucking. Expensive cosmetics that won't work and that contain massive doses of wee (disguised as urea) or snail slime; falling bum, receding gums, wrinkles, dementia.

Buying beige clothes and elasticated jeans from mail order or online catalogues. Thinking they're ATTRACTIVE.

~ ~ ~

All the articles come after this as proof, so Dad can study what they mean in the context of real-life women. I'm so wrapped up doing the cover page and gluing in the pictures that I don't know Gaffa's here until I hear whispered voices in the hall. I open up the door to listen.

(Gaffa never whispers.)

"If it's an illness," he says, "we can get it fixed."

"It's not an illness Dad. It's a condition called gender dysphoria." Dad tries to steer him into the kitchen but it's as if Gaffa has all these words to say and unless he says them now, he'll lose his nerve.

"Whatever it is, for god's sake go to Amsterdam until you've got it out of your system and don't break up this family."

Dad closes the kitchen door behind them so I creep downstairs. Wouldn't you?

"Easter," says Gaffa. "You're coming out at Easter! What are you, the second Messiah? Your mother's very upset."

"It's not 'coming out' Dad. It's becoming who I am, inside."

"Plenty of us survived wars without worrying about our insides." This isn't *exactly* what Dad was saying. "This new baby you're bringing into the world? What sort of reality will that child grow up in, Frank?"

"He or she will grow up in a happy, loving family–"

"You were born a man and that's what you were meant to be!"

Dad takes time to answer and when he does, his heart is on his sleeve but he's trying to protect it, to cover it with us. "I know it's really hard for you, as my father. I know I've disappointed you by not being the son you wanted."

He sounds tired, so very tired. "But if my kids can understand it and support me, can you not try?"

I run back upstairs and close my door tightly, leaning against it until I hear the front door. I dunno why I'm upset. It's what I wanted, isn't it? I mean this IS what I wanted.

When I've heard Gaffa's car drive off, I creep down to see how Dad is. He's decanting some frozen goujons onto an oven tray violently and doesn't turn. "Dad?" I go up beside him and he stops what he's doing, big fat tears spilling down his face. What can I do? I hug him and I hold him and let him cry.

"What would I do without you, Jessie?" he says.

TWENTY FOUR

"This is amazing!" Abby and I are sitting on the back step of our prefab. Nobody else comes here. Too many spiders. "Kind of worrying, but cool!" She's right. My survey is a disturbing compilation of how awful it is to be a woman; full of all the stuff they do NOT tell you in talks. "Think we'll go through any of this?" She makes a constipated smog monster face at the thought.

"It's useless," I say, quietly.

"What d'you mean?! Isn't this exactly what you wanted? I mean, at least now he'll make an informed choice!"

"My grandad came round last night. Told Dad that he's sick and should leave the country until he's 'cured'. The minute I give him this, he'll know I'm as bad as his own dad. That I was against it all along and I didn't tell him."

"Which is true."

This doesn't exactly help. I'm nearly in tears. Abby being Abby, puts her arm around me. "It's okay," she says. "I'm sorry. There must be something else we haven't tried."

~ ~ ~

Everyone's talking about Easter holidays. Abby's off to rellies in Cork, Alice to Spain, and Megan to New York (to an older sister), lucky gimp. Others are either visiting grandparents on farms in a Wi-Fi-swallowing abyss or lined up for camps to learn Irish or French or drama.

We'll probably spend the vacation watching Dad have tests. If we're really lucky, he'll start his hormones early and we can wait for his boobs to grow. Oh yeah, and listen to him talking about it all. By the time we go back to school, we might even have the pleasure of taking him for a walk in his first pair of outdoor heels…

I have a sudden flash image of Dad stepping into a machine and emerging as a clone of The Exorcist and only remember where I am seconds short of walking full-pelt into Alo. Scary what can happen on a school corridor when your mind is dancing on a cliff top. Wonder if that's what happens to lemmings? Are they nature's greatest daydreamers? He snarls and holds his nose as if I smell and his cronies snigger but I could care less.

Laura wants to go on retreat so now the word has spread through her disciples and up through their older sibs that we're really religious. Frankly, if we're talking religion, I prefer the idea of coming back as a really slow snail destined for a Parisian restaurant than landing up in a Heaven populated by thousands of little Laura's all irritating me at once.

Sadly, Karma makes sense. It also means that if I were to

kill Laura now, she'd come back into my next life and probably have total control. I'd be her child or something; a child that couldn't speak so I could never answer back. It's not worth it.

Our history teacher, Mr Byrne – now growing sideburns for some ungodly reason and is now no longer cute, according to Abby – has been making us work on this "exciting project" to "bring history alive". We are each designing family crests, taking account of hobbies, talents and achievements. All of 2nd Year is doing it and we'll exhibit them in the hall before we break.

"Don't hold anything back," says Mr B. "Celebrate what's unique about your family."

Great.

Wonder what he'd make of four breasts mounted on an architectural model of another breast against the backdrop of a red dress and two high heels?

The Exorcist corners me in the corridor. Apparently Nurse McCarthy asked her when the rest of our class would be in to see her as she'd like to work the individual visits into her schedule. Just my luck, it turns out the next 'talk' isn't planned until next term and my cover story is blown. The two women have concluded that my visit was a cry for help and that I need to have a confidential talk with the school counsellor (i.e. her) about "becoming a woman". Yeah and THAT'S a topic I know NOTHING about. "It's not counselling, Jessie, just a little chat." So I smile, as expected, say thank you… and I don't throw my eyes to heaven until I turn away.

~ ~ ~

"I'll fake a tummy ache. Or who knows, I might be hiding at home pretending I'm dead instead."

"You could just go?" says Abby. "Might be fun?"

I give her my best withering look as Laura bounces up. "Homework Club was cancelled but Ms O'Brien let me stay in the Chapel and pray for lost souls."

It figures. "They'll probably haunt you now." She looks at me sort of wide-eyed. I shouldn't do this. "If you haven't prayed hard enough…" But then I relent. "I'm sure you prayed more than they could have hoped for." Her face lights up so I buy her a choc ice on the way home.

"So?" says Abby. "What *are* you doing for Easter?"

"Nothing." I shrug. "We're doing nothing at all."

Dad is in the front room, singing. Well, sort of singing. Cat strangulation and boiling crabs in a big pot spring to mind but before I can see what's happening, Eva whooshes past me on her way from studio to loo.

"What's going on?"

~ ~ ~

Voice coaching.

Apparently Dad is learning to heighten and lighten his voice so he'll sound less like a man. He's a bit self-conscious about the process, Eva says, so the more we can pretend not to notice, the better. "Then, when Mandy is ready, she can surprise us."

Just like that.

So, one day soon, my dad will start talking to me in a woman's voice and I'm expected to clap my hands.

"Gaffa will come round," Eva says firmly, as if she's read my mind – she *really* hasn't – and squeezes my shoulder as. "He has to."

I trudge upstairs with Buffy while Laura goes out to play with her grave. Don't know why I got my hopes up, but what's new? There is NO WAY OUT. Get over it, I say aloud, ripping the survey apart. In certain cultures I'd be married off by now; probably the same cultures that'd stone Dad to death.

Dinosaurs had it worse. They got extinct.

Emus and kangaroos get eaten.

Might as well get used to life being one of those fun roller-coasters where you scream before you fall. And then find out it wasn't so bad, it was worse… but you can laugh about it afterwards. Once you've thrown up. Only then you discover that all your money fell out when you were upside down so you have to walk home with gooey green and yellow sick in your hair.

I get into a sort of rhythm, OBLITERATING all my hard work along with my BRILLIANT plan to solve everything. What rights do I have? I have no rights. Did I have any say about going to America, about Eva, about coming home?

About Mum dying so Laura could be born?

Speak of the devil. In swans Laura, sucking on a sherbet dip. Sherbet dips are fizzy and bitter. They are, in short, THE most amazing sweets ever invented, even counting

Tootsie Rolls. We NEVER EVER have them cos Dad and Eva both agree that sherbet dips rot your teeth.

Laura has a face on her that would be utterly saint-like if it wasn't so SMUG so I know this is no ordinary treat that Laura has wangled out of Gramma and has had hidden for weeks.

It HAS to have been a reward for something I won't like.

Cos I'm in such a snot about Dad, and Gaffa mucking everything up and now I'm remembering ALL THE WORK I put into this survey, I take it off her. I'm the older sister, see and I already got her a choc ice.

Even though I know I'll give it back, I still feel mean and that makes everything worse. "Who?"

"Alo."

I wait but she says nothing. Is there a course for training little sisters in how to be irritating? If there is – if there *was*, Laura would be top of the class. Probably is anyway. Teachers love her. "Why?"

THEN, because she loves sherbet dips more than anything in my secret box of treats and really wants this one back, Laura tells me the whole sorry tale about how she was burying Ponchinello, who didn't resurrect, despite lying on a velvet patch for two days on a shelf in the garage.

Alo poked his face over the fence because he's a troublemaker and *should know better* or maybe he was hiding from his dad's bad temper or trying to see Eva dressed as a man. Mr D. seems to be in a bad temper forever these days, I heard one of the teachers refer to him as The Grinch yesterday.

"He was asking questions about Dad but I didn't say *anything* cos you get mad when I talk about Dad but then he said he'd say a blessing over Ponchinello cos his uncle's a monk and I asked you to do it and you said no way you'd pray over an ugly killer fish–"

"What *about* Dad?"

"His dad says our dad is a *poly-gamist*," says Laura. (Which means many wives and therefore makes no sense at all.) "I said, he's not. He's a *pro-cras-tin-ator*. Which is nothing like an alligator and only means he can't be a proper man until he gets resurrected."

See why I worry?

I am the ONLY sane person in my ENTIRE family. AND I still have ALL my homework to do. I hand her back her sherbet dip and she keeps it well out of reach until there's nothing left but a sticky stick.

Life is good.

Not.

TWENTY FIVE

Jason and Alice are official and life is officially UNFAIR.

Okay so I didn't think *we'd* actually get together but still. My eyes are sore from homework and my stash of American sweets is down to single digits. I think I'm getting a sty to match the nose zit which has birthed a pair of aggressive siblings on my forehead while my rugby bruises from Monday have bruises from today to cover them.

My life is falling apart.

But that's okay since everyone thinks I'm grumpy because I'm a teenager. As if what Dad is planning has NOTHING to do with it. Trouble is, I'm running on dry. I have absolutely NO ideas left. Nobody is really on my side, except Gaffa but he doesn't know and anyway, he went about it all wrong. *I'm* not even on my side, sometimes.

Eva started mounting her work at the gallery today and with the focus on this, everything has been swept under the carpet. The bulge under said carpet is now the size of a small and very aggressive country waiting to trip us up at any moment. What's the betting it will be me who falls face first in the goo?

"Hey, Squirrel!" See, Dad has noticed nothing and nothing is getting him down. "Said we'd meet Eva at the gallery this eve. Moral support. Indian takeaway. Medical resuscitation…"

Ha ha.

~~~

"I'm sure my voice is lightening already," Dad says, breaking into *Doh-A-Deer* as we pull out. So much for being self-conscious. NOBODY should EVER sing from *The Sound of Music*. ESPECIALLY not my dad. "Well? What do my gorgeous girls think?"

"Maybe," says Laura. I stare out the window and count clouds.

Next up is *South Pacific* and Laura joins in. Then *Funny Girl*; proof that having *this dad* for *my dad* has serious drawbacks. I REALLY should not know these films. He drops me at the gallery while he and Laura go to collect the takeaway so I'm – mercifully – spared his *Wizard of Oz*.

~~~

The Merrion Gallery is carved out of two Georgian buildings down a backstreet in Dublin. "Once you find it," says the blurb on Eva's programme, "you'll return again and again," but I can think of WAY more places I'd want to return to or even *see* first. Like home. Home would be good if Laura stayed here at the gallery with Dad. Yup. That'd be perfect.

Just for a few years until I'm old enough to move away.

But Eva's work transforms spaces. Only when her sculptures and installations are gathered together do they start making sense and even a sort of deeper sense you can't put your finger on. In this Gallery, the statues we know– *Angel, Passion/Fruit* and *Ulysses* – grow powerful, the chandelier is a constellation reflecting and refracting light while her *Fallow Field* (that Dad nicknamed the *Field of Mammaries)* is a phosphorescent sea, all lit up underneath.

"Whoever gave me the dimensions of the alcoves got it wrong," says Eva. "Nothing fits where it should."

"What about swopping these two?" I suggest. "This piece doesn't even need an alcove." She agrees, which is good. Like Dad, I see indoor spaces in angles and centimetres. "If you stood *Passion/Fruit* here, she'd be a Guardian at the entrance to the show." Ten minutes later, you can see it in Eva's eyes that the whole thing will work out after all. It happens every time.

Normally it takes much longer.

I get this nasty feeling that it isn't the exhibition that's worrying her. Before I've figured out whether I WANT to know what's really bugging her, she collapses all PLONK on a nearby chair.

~~~

"I mean, I want this to happen, god knows I've wanted it all along… But what if I don't fancy him when he's a woman?"

"You could change his mind."

"You don't understand. I like men. I prefer women. Until I met your father. He was a caged bird nobody heard… and I did so want a child." She rests a hand on her stomach and takes a deep breath. "I just don't want to let your father and Mandy down."

"Eva, you HAVE to tell him."

Big mistake. I used her name. She straightens her back and shakes her head, putting me into the wrong – what's new? – and at a distance again. As if what she said didn't affect me and my ENTIRE life. Cue Dad downstairs with the largest amount of Indian takeaway ever.

Eva grabs my arm. "Not a word, Jessie."

"But Dad has a right to know if you have doubts!"

"Promise." I manage a nod. Well what would you have done!? "I'm sorry. I shouldn't have involved you. You remind me so much of your father sometimes."

I'm not sure what this means anymore.

"I'm guessing Laura takes after your mum?"

"Yeah. Yeah she does. She's just like Mum."

"I got Lamb Bhuna, Chicken Curry and Veg Biryani," says Dad. "That should be enough, shouldn't it?"

Okay, right, so I should have said something when I had the chance. But here's the thing. I don't know if Laura takes after Mum or not. I don't know if the stuff she makes up about Mum wanting her to do things or not are truer than the stuff I remember because maybe I only remember stuff because Dad told me when I was small.

But I'm the big sister, see. It was my job to remember everything for Laura cos she wasn't there and I didn't remember enough.

~ ~ ~

Salome's head is going to hit everyone over five feet tall. "That's the idea," said Eva. "I'm banging heads together."

Yeah, I didn't really get it either.

~ ~ ~

Laura falls asleep with a noodle stuck to her chin. I rearrange it to look like a cross. At least she'll wake up happy tomorrow. I decide to make myself hot chocolate in case it does actually help you sleep but half the scalding brown stuff ends up on my top because I go all clumsy lifting the drink out of the microwave.

"Boy trouble?" says Dad, appearing behind me.

That's just too ridiculous to answer.

He sticks the kettle on. "You'd tell me if you were being bullied?"

"Yup," I say, in my best crisp *not in the mood to talk* voice that NEVER works.

"Want me to make you another cup?" I shake my head. "Okee-dokeee." This is THE most annoying phrase. Second only to *Okeedokee Artichokee*.

"Eva's exhausted. She could have done with more help."

"Oh Eva likes to do it her own way."

"Not this time. As I said, she could have done with your help."

He seems surprised. Truth is, so am I. I don't USUALLY pick fights with anyone. "I've been hunting work, having tests, she knows that."

"Yeah you had tests but guess what, Eva's got a whole exhibition opening at the weekend AND she has a baby to carry AND you should have been there for her. Maybe I had a test too and you should have asked about that and about school way before now and about how Laura's settling in."

"You had tests, already?"

"No. That's not the point."

He waits. Patiently. I HATE it when he does this. Laura does it too. They wait and then you end up saying all sorts of stuff you never meant to say or shouldn't have said and it NEVER ends up good.

"We're going to lose her Dad. She's lost-er than you can imagine but you're so caught up in your own stuff, you can't see that."

He turns to the window, cradling his tea in his hands. "Thank you," he says. And I'm sorry everything's so hard for him. I'm sorry I'm so cross and I'm sorry he wants to be some other way than he is. And I think, *Yeah, right!* and *my top is ruined.* I want to hug him and say everything'll be okay but that would be a lie so I slink off to bed.

If I'd had a glass of milk instead or a mouth full of marshmallows, I couldn't have said a word.

If I'd worn another top, one I didn't like… with Laura's veil for a bib.

If I'd stayed upstairs.

Surprise, surprise, I sleep like a marmoset in a bed of honey and dream of nothing at all.

TWENTY SIX

"WHY are we going to Gramma's?"

"Dad's taking Eva out."

"They don't *usually* go out."

She's right. They stay home and drink wine and dance on the patio. "Just pack a book, your PJs and a DVD in case we have to stay over."

Tonight is my last chance to get Gramma on-side. She could persuade Dad to do stuff, or not, in a way he couldn't resist. It's always in the papers where sons say they killed or blackmailed or didn't marry someone cos their mother told them not to. Except the vampire books. Then it's an elder vampire or someone with a crucifix. Apparently crucifixes are not as effective on modern vampires though. Not the ones with golden eyes.

"You could make him stop." No, too weak. "Gramma, tell Dad he has to stop. He's too young." No, cos he's not. I'm too young. Laura's too young. Eva's unborn baby is too young! I've got it: "He's too old to be doing it now. What if it goes wrong? What if he's left being half and half and nothing?"

~ ~ ~

"Thanks Mum," says Dad. It's beginning to drizzle. The *wetting* sort of drizzle you can hardly see. "We'll only be an hour or two." There's a full moon too but that's just a crummy, mean trick to make you look up so that the drizzle can get in your eyes and down your neck.

"You take your time and no rushing back," says Gramma. "You two need some time to yourselves." See, no mention of *before you get warped into a woman* or *before you give these girls another female role model for a dad.*

"We're going to have a nice girl's night in." You can always tell when Gaffa's not in. Otherwise he's at the door, giving out to us all for letting the heat out of the house. Gaffa, she says, is out mending a burst pipe at his sister's house in Drumcondra apparently. "He'll be back soon."

She doesn't lie very well. Gaffa is avoiding Dad. That's why he's not here. It'll make it easier for me to talk to Gramma but between the taking off and hanging up of coats and Gramma hugging us – they're still the best hugs – suddenly we're sat on the sofa with two encyclopaedias on our laps. Laura's feet stick out over the edge.

When Gaffa retired, this sofa was his treat but Gramma sits on a straight-backed chair cos she has arthritis. "Occurred to me that it might help for you both of you to know your father is not the first to feel this way."

BRILLIANT.

One big happy family we will be.

"Don't you want to make us some cinnamon toast?

Laura's dying for some," I pinch Laura when Gramma's not looking so she yelps, which Gramma takes to mean yes.

"You can wait till we've had a look at these, can't you?"

Laura nods. Traitor. I'm so tired of being GRUMPY all the time. I never asked for this and before you ask, it's not hormonal. There's a steady blanketing of rain on the skylight above us, like a backdrop to a horror film.

Gramma opens a bookmarked page. "Here we are." The print is tiny. No wonder everyone needed glasses in the old days! "Colonel Sir Leslie Ivor Victor Gauntlett Bligh Barker. He was a she. Invented a convenient war wound to – you know, down there – stop questions."

"Yuk," says Laura and for once I'm with her.

It's amazing how many people Gramma has found who lived as a gender other than their own without anyone knowing or caring for entire lifetimes. The room is warm and it feels as if we're reading fairytales. But these people didn't have kids going to a local school or school principals living next door and drooling over them.

"Okay then, this is my own favourite," says Gramma."Pope Joan."

Okay, *she's* kind of cool. In a squirmy way. "That was different," I say. "She probably just wanted the job or something and only men could do it. Or she had an evil uncle who wanted to control the Pope and made her do it."

"I don't know. Story is she was a highly intelligent woman, disguised her gender for a lover and then her intelligence propelled her up the ranks of the Church. They

175

only found out she was a woman when she gave birth in a religious parade."

Gramma puts her arm around Laura, as if to comfort her for something we didn't know about till two seconds ago. "Of course they disowned her then, scratched her out of Church history. Cruel times, the Middle Ages. Can't imagine they let the baby live…"

"At least Dad can't have a baby."

I really shouldn't say things like this aloud. It's tempting fate. As soon as I say something positive in these situations, it is INEVITABLE that someone will play *squish-the-donkey* on it. Cos guess what Gramma's reply is?

"Oh I don't know love. They're making great advances every day." FAN-TAS-TIC. Does she even think about what she's saying? "Now let's see about that toast."

Poor Gramma. Sometimes I look at her and wonder what it feels like to be old and it doesn't seem fair. *This isn't some ancient war hero or crummy pope,* I want to shout. *This is my dad we're talking about.*

Instead, I lay the tray and mix the cinnamon with the sugar while Laura stays on the couch absorbed by Pope Joan. Dad says Gramma would love the internet if she gave it a chance but she won't. She likes books.

"Why are you doing this, Gramma?"

"I found it helped me accept his decision, love. I hate to think of him being so unhappy for years."

He wasn't unhappy! He had Mum. He had us. Dad only cries when he watches Bridget Jones' Diary. If he was unhappy he'd cry way more often. Besides he only cries *then* cos he has rotten taste or there's something wrong with his genes.

Oops. My genes too.

"I wish I could have been as accepting and brave as you have been," she says.

But I haven't been and I'm not. "I need to use the loo." I go upstairs and throw cold water on my face and only go down when the toast is ready.

"You okay, love?" I'm about to say, "No. No, I'm not," when she hands me a glass of warm milk to help *settle* my stomach.

"At least your Easter Holidays are coming. Lots of lazy lie-ins ahead…"

TWENTY SEVEN

"It's a political statement too," says Eva.

We're sat around the kitchen table again; Eva and Dad bouncy as bunnies. Turns out, they spent the evening in the Gallery and now Eva is removing an installation to free up a space for Dad to display his scale model and plans for the crematorium.

"After all, it is for a *national* crematorium, not a private one for the rich and very shy. Shouldn't people have some say?"

It's a fantastic idea. Dad's work's every bit as good as any artist's but nobody ever gets to see it. It's so perfect a decision that I don't even see the bombshell falling, not until it has thrown out little wiry arms and climbed onto my lap.

"We also came to another decision that your father..." She kisses him right there and then in the middle of a sentence! Get a room! "...will introduce himself to everyone on the Opening Night..."

Okay. Fine so far. What's the big deal?

"As Mandy."

"What?" Where did this come from?? See? Bombshell, bits of bloody Jessie sticking to the roof, snarling.

Woah! "You said yourself there's no rush! This is YOUR opening, Eva. What about the critics, journos?"

"I said the same thing," says Dad. "But we talked it through and about how you tackled O'Grady and told your grandparents and how strong you've been from the start." He's smiling at me. Why is he smiling at me?

"So I thought, damn it, if my little Squirrel can tell people to go to hell… then I can do this. No more lies. No going back."

"You did a very brave thing, telling your father how I felt," says Eva. "You took a risk for the sake of all of us. You have been braver than either of us."

Suddenly I'm complicit. It's ALL my fault.

"Oh Jessie," says Dad. "Don't you see? It's because of you that we have the courage to do this!"

Eva hammers in the final coffin nail. "We'll show the world, as a family, in public, that we're not ashamed of your father, Mandy. We're proud." Then there's the ubiquitous group hug during which everyone notices that it's way past Laura's bed time but I go too cos the alternative is to sit up with Dad and Eva being all lovey dovey and hatching their plans for a world takeover.

"So much to do before Saturday," says Dad.

"Sure."

I close the door on them. *I could run away, change my name, become an invisible ankle-biting gnome.* Buffy waits at the top of the stairs with a big wide-eyed look of sympathy.

~ ~ ~

"D'you think the new baby will call Dad, Dad or Mum?"

"Eva will be Mum. Dad will be…" I can't bear to say it.

"Mandy!"

"Yeah," I say, through gritted teeth. Never understood that expression before but yup, you couldn't get air past these teeth tonight.

I lie awake, listening to Laura sleep. Getting up and doing something else feels pointless, even if I never sleep again. It's the perfect night for a storm to rip the sky apart and drown out all the thoughts firing around my head but that's as useless as wishing I hadn't said anything to Dad last night.

When I finally sleep, I'm swallowed into a long tunnel that keeps getting thinner, the walls pressing in. When I try to scream, clouds come up from under my feet and I'm choking on them. I wake Laura up in time for school and remember it isn't a *dream* I need to worry about. our dad is 'coming out' publicly as Mandy on Saturday.

In two days time.

Laura chatters; I stay mute but that's okay. She once told me it doesn't matter if nobody listens. The point, for her, is the saying of the words. She has now decided that she wants to be a pope as well as a saint and a nun. I tell her she can't.

"Popes are men."

"Pope Joan was a pope."

"By pretending to be a man. Besides, you'd have to be a priest first and you can't be a priest."

Which gets me TOTALLY off subject cos she says, "Why can't I be a priest?"

"You just can't, that's why! Cos priests are men too."

~ ~ ~

"What's up?" says Abby, when we call for her to go to school.

It's a beautiful day. Clear skies. Not a patch of cloud. A perfect day for feeling down. "Worst yet," I say and fill her in as we go down the hill to school.

"Least they sorted themselves out," she says. "You helped them and that's good."

I HATE having an optimist for a friend.

~ ~ ~

Mr O'Byrne gives us an hour in the afternoon to work on our 'Family Crest'. Since all I've done is paint the shield red, he suggests I list family members and what I know about them to see if it throws up any ideas for images to include.

So I do. Dad's grandparents were cobblers, so I draw a shoe. A veil for Laura, a cat for me. Gaffa gets a panther and Gramma hands, for her hugs. Mr B. points out that I've filled in three generations but have somehow left out my parents.

"It's a bit complicated, Mr O'Byrne," says Abby.

It's best to say nothing. I could have told her that. Now he'll want to know and then the class will listen in and everything will get worse.

"Really," he says. "Well then, how about you just draw an actual tree joining all the images; the tree can be the family as a whole?" Strangely enough, nobody says a thing. Nobody teases or quizzes me.

"Cheer up," says Abby. "You can take it all out on Alo at rugby."

She's right. When I'm on the pitch, even if I'm only doing laps, I can forget everything else.

"Wonder if I should warn him?"

I'm barely listening. Out on the pitch, it's just me and my body and focussing on doing my best. Rugby requires brains. Not the emotional, doubtful type but the sort that sees a gap, tabulates a speed and an angle and who to pass to. You don't get to think and when you're done, you're too tired to worry about anything.

So I cheer up and say, "Yeah. Maybe you should warn him!"

And that is probably why heavy thundery clouds roll up out of nowhere, dangle themselves like grumpy toffee apples over the rugby pitch and rip themselves into torrents of rain mid-afternoon; rain heavy enough to float an Ark.

The rugby pitch is flooded and practice is cancelled.

Lucky Alo.

~ ~ ~

Laura wore trousers to school today instead of the skirt. Fortunately nobody noticed that she was now "being a man" as well as a saint-in-making and a nun cos in junior school – another example of life's unfairness – you can wear either.

"Don't be stupid. You can't just become a man."

"Why not? If Dad can be a girl. 80% of saints are men anyway."

I don't want to know where she got this fact or who she might have asked. "You have to grow up first. If they did it now, you'd probably die. Horribly."

"Like a martyr." Laura brightens as if she were a little light bulb plugged into the sun. Of course, the sun came out again as soon as practice was cancelled but does it soak up the rain? Not a bit. We trudge home through globulous puddles. Such a waste of a Friday evening.

"I think I might put a nodding dog on my crest, sitting on knitting needles," says Abby.

"Your dad would LOVE that."

"Exactly."

The trees alongside the pavement unleash the rain they clasped to their bushy hearts. We are as wet as water-muffins before we've even reached the hill.

"You do *know* Jason fancies you," says Abby.

"As in Jason who is going out with Alice?"

"I don't think he knew he was going out with her until she told everyone and now he's probably afraid to break it off with her. She freaked when Mike dumped her and shredded all his hardbacks."

"Boys are stupid," I say.

"Except Jason."

I nod. "Maybe." I have to give him that.

"She'll dump him eventually." If I lost both legs, Abby would say, "At least you have your arms".

I can see it all now, even if Abby can't. *Hi Jason, want to meet my dad? Isn't his dress divine? Helped him pick it myself. I wonder if you'd like to have a dance with him if he promises not to bite?* Still, I guess it's nice to think he doesn't see me as a weirdo dork.

Yet.

~ ~ ~

Dad's deciding between red and black backing board for his plans. The model is already tucked into a box, complete with a miniature coffin and trees, to bring into the gallery.

"Dad, can I talk to you?"

"Sure." He plumps for the black mounting board and starts gluing it up.

Where do I start? How can he be so calm? *Talk to him,* that's what Abby said. "You're making a mistake." There. It's said. The sky hasn't fallen down. I haven't self-combusted into a puddle of ash.

"Red. You think I should use the red?"

He thinks I'm talking about the backing board! Why am I even trying?

"You know, you're absolutely right. That's my Squirrel! Always cutting straight through the problem to the solution."

"Don't think so, Dad. "

"So, what do you want to talk about? I promised Eva I'd get this into the gallery by four for the photo shoot–"

"It's four now."

"Oh dear!" He's on his feet, handing me the box and grabbing his keys. "I'll be an hour max. We'll talk then, okay? And don't open the door to anyone, okay. Don't even answer the phone. Unless it's me. Or Gramma. Definitely not if it's a five-headed dragon or a giant snake."

"I'm not a kid."

He goes all soft at the edges. "I know, love. I know. You remind me so much of your mum sometimes." He hugs me quickly, as if it still hurts a bit and I help him load his work into the car.

"Where's he going?" says Laura.

"He's going to build an orchestra pit on the moon."

"Will he stay over?"

"No, he'll be home before you go to bed."

I make her cheesy pasta and tell her I need our bedroom to myself for a little while.

~ ~ ~

Clouds change, says Dad, but he's wrong. They don't *change* and STAY clouds. I pull all the pieces of my survey out of the bin and start piecing them together. See, with clouds, there's this big deadly dance goes on when hot air meets cold air and turns to rain. Then you have wetness and sadness and people feeling sore for no good reason except they're wet and miserable. And everyone says that's just how it is and no-one else sees a problem.

After all, it's only rain.

I stick all the pages into a giant scrapbook and glue a great big cotton wool cloud to the front. Cos that's what he doesn't get: Clouds don't change; they *disappear*. Everything you knew and loved vanishes in one wet swoop.

Nothing can ever be *the same*.

Dad doesn't make it home until after seven. We watch a

Harry Potter film and he falls asleep on the couch. His last night as an almost-normal-Dad.

I dream of being encased in cement and force-fed broccoli but I wake to a crisp dawn.

Saturday.

The Day of Judgement.

TWENTY EIGHT

I take the deepest breath imaginable to try and stop my whole body shaking with nerves. ETM – *Estimated Time to Mandy* – seven hours and counting. What's Dad doing with these crucial hours? He's making pizza!

"Thought we could eat early, get in and help Eva out for the last few hours."

How can he be so calm?

Laura's outside heave-rolling a heavy pot plant across the patio so I don't have to bribe her to stay out of hearing. This is the Last Manoeuvre of the Desperate Daughter. "Dad," I blurt, holding out the survey. "Before it's too late–"

He wipes his hands on a tea towel covered with yellow chickens. "What's this? Finally asking for the benefit of my wisdom on a school project?!"

"It's about you. What you're doing." He takes it from me as if it were the Book of Kells. "What I said I wanted to talk to you about. Yesterday. Before you went out. I'll go check on Laura."

I flee into the garden before he realises what he's holding;

my nerve is shot. "Where do you want it?" I say, picking up the pot.

~~~

How Dad dug a grave for her little venomous fish without noticing the Laura-sized one nearby and suggesting it might be a LITTLE bit odd is beyond me. She has lined the inside with an old sheet from the studio and placed three potted plants along the side. The clouds in the sky do not promise rain.

Pity.

"We do this once, that's all." Anything to stay out of the house.

Laura nods, hands me her bible and hops down into the grave like a little gerbil. Lying down, she folds her hands prayerfully and settles her face into what she assumes is a saint-like expression.

I open the Bible at random. "*For behold, the Lord will come with fire and with his chariots as a whirlwind…*" I read as flatly as I can, but the language of it sort of takes over. It's fun pretending to be a preacher and my voice rises up… "*To render his anger with fury and his rebuke with flames of fire…*"

"You burying your sister?" says a voice from atop the wall. Alo. Of course it's Alo.

"You want to be next?" The head disappears.

"*For by fire and by his sword will the Lord plead with all flesh and the slain of the Lord…*" This is SO not appropriate. Perhaps that's why it's fun. "Will I go on?"

"Yes please," says Laura.

Seven verses later, I realise I should be there for Dad to help him cope with his change of heart. I abandon Laura in her makeshift grave, looking all peaceful with the bible on her tum. She says she wants to be alone. The grave is only as deep as my knees and the excavated earth is well back. Alo will probably hop over to help her out anyway.

Spooky, she seems to have got a boyfriend, albeit a weird one, before I have.

"It's okay," I practice, heading inside. "Better now than later." I will admit that I should have said something, right at the start but that I didn't want to hurt him and whatever he decides, I'll support him.

The kitchen's full of smoke. I'm rescuing the pizza when I hear him in the hall.

"Can you imagine the effort it took?"

I open the door slowly. Dad's on the phone, with his back to me, the scrapbook open in his hand.

"Yeah, I thought I'd ring Dr Strauss and tell her. Can't imagine she's come across anything like this before." Before I can to close the door quietly, he gestures me forward. "Great work love. Really impressed! Eva thinks you're amazing too! But then she always did!"

Then he's back on the phone. "But listen, it's given me an idea."

He likes it. My idiot Dad thinks I did this survey to help him. I head upstairs. I've no appetite for partially-incinerated pizza anyway.

"What if we do a sort of family-change book; call it *Make Me A Mermaid Too...* The girls could keep diaries of their thoughts, experiences, questions; we could keep track of everything related to it that we see in the papers…What's wrong with the title?"

I empty the folder Dad gave me into my bag to dump at school. If I bin them here, he'll only find them and want to know why. The stupid print-outs and the idiot leaflets and goody good questionnaire. Then I move the calendar over to Laura's wall. I don't want to know what's happening next cos it just keeps getting worse and worse anyway.

Dad's back in the kitchen calling Laura in when I go down so I grab my coat and leave. I can't sit across from Dad with him beaming at me as if I've done something really good when I haven't. I don't want to go in and help Eva play happy families and I do NOT want to be there when Dad's getting ready for the exhibition.

When *Mandy* asks me which dress to wear.

TWENTY NINE

"Please. I don't want to be at home right now." I forgot people 'do' weekends differently here. They have family time and meal times and you don't just drop in unannounced. "Couldn't you say you asked me over and forgot to tell them?"

Abby knows I'm serious. I can see her brain ticking over, how to make this okay.

"There's no-one in the house and I lost my key?"

She nods. "Leave it to me but stick close behind and overhear *everything*. They hate being rude even more than they hate uninvited guests!"

~ ~ ~

"She's a bit nervous in case it's a flop cos she really loves Eva and she'd hate to see it go wrong. And it has done, sometimes, cos her stuff can be really controversial. In Texas they had guns and wanted to smash everything up. But she can't say anything cos how could she? So it's really awkward to be at home with her dad right now though he's probably worried too cos when he worries, he keeps insisting everything going to be fine."

Mrs D. looks over at me. I hang my head and look ashamed. It isn't difficult since that's *exactly* how I feel. Then I help Abby lay an extra place at the table while her Mum phones Dad. "Yes, we were surprised too. But it's so lovely for them to be friends, don't you think?"

She wipes floury hands on flowery apron and smiles to let me know she's not going to give the game away. "Well, this'll give you one less thing to worry about. She can have lunch here and we'll drop her into the Gallery for six."

Half of me hopes Dad will say, *No, I want her to come in with me* but he's so caught up in everything to do with today that he probably won't even notice I'm not there.

~ ~ ~

"Want to talk?"

"Not yet."

Right now, I want to pretend I live in a normal family with normal parents. I'll even take the Warthog for a brother if I must. I don't mind the way Mrs D. fusses over her kids; it's kind of nice, even if Alo most DEFINITELY isn't worthy. Maybe he was left here by a stray cuckoo or Abby's mum looked at a wasp's nest just before giving birth but she only sideways, with one eye and so Abby wasn't affected.

Mr D. carves. Though the roast is the size of a guinea pig, he makes it look as if it were manly work. Mrs D. has made rhubarb crumble and custard with a choice of cream or custard.

So here it is, my fantasy: Dad is Dad. He comes home in a three-piece suit and pipe and never changes into a dress or a twin-piece or plait his hair. "I'm home," he says and we all run into his arms. Laura hasn't dug herself a grave in the back garden cos that would be weird and he'd be worried.

We have family meals of meat and veg and potatoes and he makes sure we don't stay up late. After he tucks us in, he hangs our uniforms by the heater so they'll be warm and in the morning, we all have breakfast together. We bring lunches to school that Dad made the night before and they are never Tikka Marsala, refried beans or pizza sandwiches.

"I tried to talk to him," I whisper while we wash up. The warmth of the water seeps into me. "I gave him the survey."

"And?"

"He thought I was trying to help him become a woman."

~ ~ ~

"You must be so proud of her," says Mrs D. "Whatever the critics say, that is what you hold onto."

"Yes Mrs D."

She smiles. Job well done, child reassured, she opens the hall door. The whole Darcy family has decided to come to the launch to show their support.

The neatest little rain cloud sits above the car; PERFECT as a getaway if I could only reach high enough. Abby's mum seems surprised by it. "They said it wouldn't rain today," she says to no one in particular and insists on lending me a coat.

"I don't think you should go." Everyone turns and stares. I didn't mean it to come out so loud. "The opening, it'll be full of Eva's arty friends. It's not as if her work will 'go off' or anything. No 'Best Before' on Eva's shows!"

But when was the last time anyone listened?

"Or you could drop me off and go have some nice family outing somewhere else? You could go some other time, when it's quieter. I mean, it's on for two whole weeks, right through Easter."

"Don't be silly," says Mrs D. "We're all looking forward to it."

This is clearly an example of her talking for everyone else. Alo has been dragged into a suit as if he were being forced to join a cult and Mr D. has already knocked back two brandies pretending they were medicinal and straightened his tie five times. Maybe he's not so confident when he's not bossing children about.

"It'll be fine," says Abby, before Alo squishes into the back of the car with us. I sit very still and stare out front.

~~~

The gallery is SWARMING despite the fact that it's 6pm on a Saturday. Eva glows at the centre of it all; mingling, lingering, keeping an eye on everyone she has to talk to. An Opening is usually when you sell most stuff, so it's looking good. Dad says she morphs like a chameleon flower into *exactly* the artist from whom each individual wants to buy work. At some exorbitant price.

Everyone's clutching a glass of wine. Two have already bumped heads with Salomé and they won't be the last. It lightens the atmosphere, adding slapstick and laughter. I'm surprised half her work isn't doused in wine but I guess these people are used to waving their arms around while holding glasses.

Mr D. spots several celebrities and heads off, beaming like a fire engine. Abby and I head in the opposite direction. If he gets to talk to any of them, his siren will go off. We do NOT want to be held responsible. Nor do we want to be called in as witnesses! Laura's with Gramma over by Dad's exhibit. It looks good. Gramma has Laura's veil and halo in her hand. I'm not sure how. There's no sign of Gaffa but then I wasn't really expecting he'd be here.

Alo gravitates with his camera towards the crematorium. A new sensitive side to The Beast? Apparently not. As we pass, we hear him talking to a guy in a Stetson. "I mean, one thing to live surrounded by breasts, but to be buried in one would be savage!"

Nope. The Monster/Warthog/Neanderthal Man is alive and well.

There's no sign of Dad or Mandy in either room."Maybe he's changed his mind," hisses Abby. "It's a scary crowd." I cross my fingers and I'm thinking, *hoping* she's right when we come face to face with a tray of scampi.

"Hi, Jessie." It's Jason. "Abby." Of course. His uncle's catering business must be doing this event. I dislike scampi intensely but take three pieces and gobble them down with a great big, "Yum". WHAT is the matter with me?! Then he gets called away.

He said MY name first, I think, dishonourably.

"Told you," says Abby.

"I feel sick."

We're heading for the toilet when we spot Mr D. standing on his own. Abby says this is odd. He's also looking shifty. We're moving away before he spots us when Dad – *Mandy* – emerges from the bathroom. Before we can blink, Mr D. slaps a hairy paw on Mandy's left buttock. GROSS. He was lying in wait!

"Dad!" Abby zones in with the sting of a bee.

Mr D. leaps back, as if he'd been caught stealing milk from a baby, trips over something invisible to us which could be a shoelace or a mischievous elf and before he knows which side is up, he's spinning into a nosedive. If it weren't for Dad catching him, he'd have landed headfirst in Eva's *Fallow Field*.

As it is, cameras flash from every angle, capturing Mandy and George in an awkward embrace.

"I'm so sorry Jessie." Mrs D. grabs her husband by the arm and steers him towards the exit. "Never used to be this way… It's that school. He should never have been made Principal…" Alo and Abby follow. "Told you the pressure would be too much but did you listen? Did you?"

Then it's Dad and me surrounded by the buzz of everyone half-looking and laughing and working out what just happened.

"It wasn't my fault," he says.

I hardly hear him. Mandy looks beautiful. Not like my dad at all. I wipe a squidge of mascara from his nose. HOW does he always get it on his nose? I mean, that takes SKILL! Then Eva taps her microphone for silence and everyone swells into the main room like obedient hounds. We step back, out of the way; not great crowd people, Dad and I.

"Ladies and gentlemen," she begins, "chosen guests and friends, boys and girls and everything in between. Tonight is a bit of a double whammy for me and my partner. As well as introducing you to my work, *Gender: The Great Divide and the Great Equaliser*..." Cue applause, bravos and whistles... "and one of my partner's myth-making architectural designs." More applause.

Dad grips my hand.

"...We have chosen tonight to mark the transformation of the love of my life into Mandy, the woman he has always believed himself to be."

"Wish me luck," he whispers as Eva holds out a hand and he – pooooof – SHE steps through the parting sea of spectators to take it.

"Honoured Guests, the woman I fell in love with six years ago: Mandy Keane."

My dad.

THIRTY

It's done. Dad is out as Mandy. It's almost a relief. I sleep like a sloth drunk on hot milk and honey, waking often but only long enough to remember I'm in bed and cosy before drifting back to sleep. I dream of nothing at all.

When I finally wake up, I lie there for ages wondering why there's no sense of dread and then I remember: *it's done.*

And Jason knew my name!

Eva sends me down to buy the Sunday papers. She wants to see what coverage the exhibition got. It's a beautiful day. Crisp, clear sky. Small fluffy clouds without a hint of grey. The worst is over. I mean, what else can happen now?

So I'm trotting down the hill, smiling at dogs peeing in gardens and barking in yards. I'm thinking that the sky seems bigger today as I wait for the lights to change at the bottom of the hill. There's even the hint of a fluffy elephant in the clouds above the shops, 'cept it has three legs, spiky ears and the smallest snout an animal could have and still be able to smell.

I cross over, feeling relieved that I'm able to see shapes in the clouds again. Then I spot Mr D. at the news stand, between me and the shop entrance. He's leafing through papers with a face on him so sour I can smell it from 20 metres. I try to pass by, real quiet, avoiding eye contact and definitely NOT looking for trouble – or interaction, ANY interaction – when he turns and corners me with the *Sun*. Not the hot thing, that'd mean he was a wizard or something. Just the paper. But it's pretty intimidating, for a tabloid, when it's being waved in your face and he's RAGING.

I don't see much of the text but there's a photo of him and Mandy framed against a field of under-lit ceramic breasts. The title, 'School Head Saved From Field of Boobs', leaps off the page with a yip and a bounce and a 'come get me' sort of attitude.

"Your '*father*' did this deliberately!"

"I'm sure he didn't," I say, folding up the newspaper and handing it back to him.

Mr D. takes a deep breath and turns a lighter shade of blood pressure. I try to move past him into the shop. He's having none of it. "Of course," he says. "Walk with me."

And so I end up heading home again without even getting *into* the shop.

"You're a bright girl Jessie," he says.

NEVER trust an adult who says this. What follows is rarely good.

"None of this is your fault, is it? Caught in the middle of his exhibitionist game… You tried to warn us not to go to the launch, didn't you? That was resilient… and brave. Oh yes. It takes a lot of bravery to stand up to your parents and

Abby's your friend, isn't she? So you wouldn't want anything to come between the two of you."

He presses the button for the lights and ushers me across the road before I even know what's happening. "Not when you're new in town."

Why didn't I stay in bed? I could be under my duvet right now, asleep or even half asleep, or eating breakfast. Even if it was Dad's crummy porridge, I wouldn't mind today. "Dad's not hurting anyone," I try. We're already heading up the hill.

"Is he not?" Mr D. stops dead and turns full face to me. "Is he not?"

It's as if I'm in a bad sci-fi movie when the camera stops on a face for a reaction but nothing happens for the longest time. Then, when you're not expecting it, an eyebrow leaps or a knife comes down and everyone shrieks. Only then someone says, *Ach I knew that was going to happen; I wasn't scared!* But they were. Given the colour of his face, maybe there's an alien inside Mr D. that's going to burst forth.

All that will be left of me for the forensic detectives to find will be a sliver of disgorged entrails by the wheelie bin of number 24.

"Are *you* not hurting, Jessica?"

I can't meet his eyes. He shouldn't ask me now, not when it's too late, not in a kind voice that makes it seem as if he really cares. Why the hell did I have to get up so early? As for fetching the papers, I could have said, "Laura'll go," cos she's always good for an errand, given she's trying to be holier than thou and put others first.

"It's done now," I manage.

"Could be undone," he says, ever so quietly. This is daft. It can't be undone. So why do I feel as if, for a moment, he's offering to turn back time? This sneaky, dislikeable man isn't finished yet. "You would prefer if he stopped, wouldn't you?"

Again with the *kind* voice! This isn't how Principal Darcy speaks. It's like having a devil sitting on top of your head pulling out hedgehog spikes you didn't even know were there because he wants to take your headache away.

"Before it's too late."

So I nod. Because it's true and nobody has asked me before. He starts walking again, as if it's the most natural thing in the world for me to stroll home with the father of my best friend.

"I can help you do that Jessie but you have to trust me."

And then there's Mandy, pulling the trash bin down the side so it's ready for tomorrow. "Hi George," he says, all neighbourly. "Fancy a coffee?"

It's all there in how Mr Darcy reacts. The straightening of his shoulders. The pulling in of all his face muscles to prevent a sneer. The formal, "Not right now. Thank you."

"Where're the papers?" says Dad as I go in.

I manage a shrug and trudge upstairs and back to bed.

"Hey Eva, guess what this girl did? Went all the way down to the shop and forgot…"

You can guess the rest.

HA HA.

THIRTY ONE

"Ready?"

It's a redundant question. Laura is always ready for school. She's ready before I've even woken up but this time I grab my coat and she has to catch up with me.

"Don't you want to call for Abby?"

"No." I have no idea what lies ahead today but it can't be good. There's no point calling for Abby when her dad's there but I don't want to spoil Laura's day.

She keeps looking at me crookedly through her veil so I tell her all about odd Easter traditions such as sucking an egg out of its shell through a tiny pin hole so you can roll the empty egg down a hill without getting scrambled egg inside. Painting egg shells so that the poisonous paint can seep into the egg and give people tummy ache. And yes, I've got it all mixed up but it stops her looking at me.

"I could be the Patron Saint of Easter," she says with a grin.

"Think that post went to the guy who got resurrected a while back."

"Patron Saint of Easter Bunnies then. Or of Kids Who Don't Get Easter Eggs."

"Why not?" I say. Might as well be that as anything else. "Want to meet for lunch?" She shakes her head. Having spotted some of her disciple half way down the hills, she's itching to get away from Big Sis. "Anyone says anything, you tell them to talk to me."

"Sure," she says, not listening, and wiggles off into happiness.

My school's pretty empty when I go in. Except for loners like me. That's the good thing about going in early.

Maybe those Pagan gods have finally decided to help me out because even as the school fills up, no-one's talking what happened at the Gallery. Perhaps everyone's too grumpy to bother or none of them read newspapers.

Either is fine.

Still, I don't really exhale till little break, which is when I see the notice board. Someone has stuck up the newspaper pic of George and Mandy and added a love heart around their heads. I tear it down and don't care who sees. Which is good as there must be twenty people there, all trying to take photos of the cutting on their phones and thinking it's a great big joke to see the Principal being held in the arms of a woman who isn't his wife.

"Yes. It's hilarious. Really *REALLY* funny. I mean, there couldn't be anything funnier than a man in a dress, could there!"

"Wow," says Jason. I didn't even see him standing there. "That told them."

"What?"

He puts his hands up and backs away as if I were blowing fire from my nostrils which I would, if I could. "Not armed. Honestly. Look!" He smiles. "Even my vampire teeth are withdrawn."

I turn and walk away.

"See?" I say to Abby when she catches up. "Even he's laughing at me." What does it matter now anyway?

"They didn't make the connection," says Abby. "No-one knows Mandy's a man."

"Are you serious?!" I wish she'd stop trying to cheer me up.

"They didn't connect Mandy with you either. Not till you told them, if then."

"Big deal. Alo will tell them, soon as his brain wakes up. Bound to have taken pictures. Maybe he stuck up that cutting!"

"It's his dad too, remember, so I doubt it."

How stupid was I to think I could start again in this country with its cold weather and rain and Dad being Dad. If her father hadn't acted like a lovesick wolfhound, mine wouldn't be pinned to the school notice board.

"Hey!" She grabs my arm to stop me disappearing into the bathroom. "Shouldn't I be mad too? I mean, *your* dad did turn *my* dad into a laughing stock in public."

"Well then he shouldn't have been pinching other women's bums, should he?" I'm sorry the minute it's out and I say so.

She's not convinced. "He could lose his job over this."

"I'm being horrible. I don't mean to be horrible. It's

just… I'm so fed up with being the one everyone thinks is weird. Your dad, he didn't do anything wrong, not really. I mean, not *majorly* wrong. What he did is normal, sort of, I mean compared to Dad. To *Mandy*."

"Tell that to Mum. She has him sleeping on a pull-out in Moodge's room." The idea of Abby's Dad camping in a room filled with nodding-headed-dogs makes us both smile, for a moment. "Threw out all his brandy too."

Seems fair enough."You want to come back after rugby?"

"I daren't," says Abby. "He's really mad. Made me promise not to talk to you but then…" She grins but it's a sad sort of grin "…It's not as if he can really tell me what to do now. Mum'll just bark at him!" She doesn't say anything for a while and then she adds, "Your dad – *Mandy* – looked great," she adds, "by the way."

~ ~ ~

Abby was right. Everyone's curious about what Mr D. was doing, not about the woman he was with and it's Abby who gets the hard time. I tell them all to back off. Alo comes out barking like a guard dog telling everyone it's none of their business so it's clear he hasn't told anyone who Mandy is either.

It's probably embarrassing enough that your dad publicly made a pass at a woman that wasn't your mum and that the picture got in the newspaper, without saying he fancied a gender-transitioning 'man'.

In Geography, we present our projects on Death. Mine is at home, unfinished but it turns out Mr Lynch doesn't make it past H in the alphabet so I have till Wednesday. Alo used photos of Dad's model of the crematorium. Mr Lynch is impressed until Alo gives his interpretation. "Neolithic burial mounds were shaped like breasts so we can be spewed to the gods in, like, a jet of breast milk or something."

~ ~ ~

"Did you know my dad fancied Mandy?" Abby says between classes. "Alo says you did and that's why you didn't want Mum n Dad to go to the Opening."

"How could I have?" I can hardly tell her he was ogling Mandy over the wall without making her feel worse. Sometimes little lies are good. Fluffy white ones; rain-free clouds. "I just didn't want them to see Dad coming out as Mandy."

"Fair enough."

"You okay?"

She's been on trial all day. "Mum says she wants to move."

"Move? Where?" She shrugs, but doesn't look me in the eye. "You can't leave!"

"Would I have a choice?" Her phone rings. "Did you? About coming here?"

THIRTY TWO

Jesus clicks his fingers at me. Abby hasn't shown up and he's lost patience. "Take Abby's place mid-field." He'll never know how much I absolutely need the mud n sweat today, nothing to think about except getting the ball through. Out on the field, everyone is flesh and bone, nothing else; nobody cares who I am, what happened on Saturday night or who my dad is.

Near half time, I reckon I can score. I'm primed to prove I deserve to play in this position when a vision arrives. When I say 'vision', that's way more positive than I feel , but judging by the head-spin Jesus manages, it sums up what Jesus thinks he has seen.

Dad has come to my rugby practice as Mandy. He's wearing a Dublin t-shirt but there's still way too much cleavage. (In my book, ANY is way too much.) Jesus is mesmerised. Before I can react, the ball lands in my arms. Foolishly, I freeze. Next thing I know, my only view of the world is from under ten sweaty bodies.

The whistle blows and I've missed my chance to shine.

It's my own fault. Before everything happened, maybe a week and a half ago, I told Dad our team was rubbish. I was REALLY fed up. I'd only played for three minutes at the end of a league match because of injuries and then we scored an own goal. A really stupid own goal. It wasn't my fault but I felt it as if it was.

So maybe I over-egged it a little but Dad being Dad took it that we WERE the worst, as in falling off the scales in terms of BADNESS and getting mauled by piranha dogs on the way down. Since the smell of blood would bring in the rest of the pack, you'd be luxury, extra chunk dog-meat before you hit the bottom.

Not that there would be much of you. To hit the bottom or anything else.

'Cept maybe a very *clean* skeleton…

The onion that encloses me unpeels. Alo, amazingly, puts out a hand to help me up but I hardly notice. Thanks to the scrum, there's so much mud in my hair and on my face, that I could be a smog monster birthed by the gloam. I'm pretty certain even Dad won't be able to pick me out but just in case, I volunteer to chop oranges and set to, keeping out of sight.

I have to get my story straight in case someone makes the connection, in case Dad says something. If I severed a finger, I doubt I'd notice

"Mandy," I'll say. "She's … my father's sister, cousin, *twin!* Twin *clone*. They were part of a GMO experiment. Modified pesticides." Yeah. Perfect. Nobody will see through that! "Hardly know her at all. Dad's family. Not ours. Barely knows my name!"

"Hey, Jessie!" Big bear wave from Mandy. Lots of body movement. Double D. Clearly Dad decided not to listen to Eva, though she was right. Double D looks WAY wrong.

"She's the twin we try to hide," I say to no one in particular, waving back. Well you have to. If I didn't wave, Dad would think I was ignoring him and come straight over. Fortunately, Jesus has no intention of setting him free.

"Hey." Rick, one of Alo's gang, grabs the last whole orange out of the bag. "*Cool* Mum." Rick NEVER takes orange. He's the one who can play the tin whistle with his nose and burp his ABC's. Apparently. "I mean scary... but cool."

Before I can react, Rick bounces back on to the pitch to show off some fancy footwork. Presumably to impress 'her'.

Abby appears at my shoulder. "Clearly didn't read your guidebook."

"What?"

"The heels. I mean, there was so much in that survey we did about how bad high heels are, though it's pretty amazing that he can balance. I guess they're sort of symbolic."

Oh enough of the understanding. "It wasn't a guidebook. It was a warning..."

"That's what I meant, but isn't that what your dad thought it was?"

I shrug. She's right. Dad thought it was a Guide to Womanhood. Clever me. "Where were you?"

"Had to see Dad. Mum was worried cos he wasn't returning her calls but he's okay. Licking his wounds and catching up on sleep and paperwork in the office. He wanted to vent for a while and I didn't think I could leave until he was done."

Jesus strolls over. "You," he says to Abby, "are late."

"Women's problems," she says, quick as a flash. "See when I have my period, they can be really heavy–"

"Enough." He's gone green along the gills but maybe it's a reflection of our rugby kit. He toys with a fragment of orange rind as if it were something precious and keeps his eyes on Mandy the whole time. "When exactly your mother played?"

Oops.

"I don't remember Ireland, you had women's rugby?"

Nope, I wasn't expecting that question. Twin clones won't cover it.

"In the 80s," says Abby. "Only lasted a year or two. Sponsorship dried up."

But I'm hardly listening cos over there, by the sideline, Mandy is accepting an isotonic drink from Alice. This can only mean that Alice is shaping up to ask Mandy something. I walk in their direction at Wild Cat Scent-of-Blood speed…and maybe I have suddenly acquired a superhuman power because I'm sure I can hear Alice say to my dad, "*You look amazing, what steroids are you on?*"

"Not *exactly* steroids," says Mandy.

"Uh oh," says Abby, hot on my heels.

Understatement of the year. I have to stop Mandy before Dad explains they're female hormones… It's not as if Mandy is really Dad. At least, it doesn't feel as if it's Dad that I'm propelling myself towards at speed, powered by my entire body, spirit and soul. But it *is* a world-class tackle, the best I've ever done… and down Mandy goes. Down, down, off his high-heeled stoops and into the mud.

Unfortunately, up goes a 'chicken fillet' – one of those silicone things Dad puts in a bra to give himself breasts; yeah, YUCK. It flies into the air by some propulsion I began when I grabbed his waist. By instinct, all the players standing on the pitch launch themselves upwards, as if it's a throw-in.

I've never seen them leap so high but it flies through their hands like a jello rocket. Before anyone can see what it was, this dog that's been lurking around snaps it up and runs. I love dogs!

Jesus is over in a heartbeat, helping Mandy up. "What was that?!"

"That… was my daughter," says Mandy-Dad but I'm sooo not in the mood for him to be proud of me right now. I'm out of there.

I'm probably off the team and I don't even care anymore.

~ ~ ~

I grab my bag from the changing room and go straight to Laura's Homework Club. "Mum said she wanted us to come home early today," I say to the teacher in charge. Well you get tired of saying step-mum all the time. I glare up at some fluffy shapeless clouds while I wait. "Thanks a bunch. You're meant to warn me of natural disasters in my life."

Laura bounces out. "Nice look." Yeah, mud from head to toe was always a good look for me.

Home is empty, which is a relief. Eva's in the gallery and

Dad, well I imagine Mandy's still flirting with my Brazilian coach which will be gossip enough until someone notices his Adam's Apple despite the scarf or matches her to the woman holding Mr D. on the notice-board. I feed Laura and release her into the wild, i.e. the back garden, to play with her grave.

"If anyone asks, I have my period."

"Again?"

"Yeah. So I'm going to bed now. And if I don't get left alone for a very long time, I kill someone. Slowly. "

"You should shower first," she says.

Grrr.

THIRTY THREE

The yard is full of odd looks and furtive whispers, as if hundreds of eyes are zoned in on us but nobody says a word and Alo is nowhere to be seen. Laura takes my hand before we go through the gates. She knows all about the rugby by then. I had to tell her so she'd understand what happens next.

Sometimes I love her to bits.

Words you can react to or at least understand but you can't really answer a 'look' cos you don't know what they're *really* thinking or what was said that made this look appear. Anything you say in defence of what they might be thinking or saying makes you look paranoid and weird.

It should be water off a crane's bum but it feels worse here somehow and I didn't think that was possible. Laura's still with me when I bump into Alice and her gang. They have their backs to us, except Megan who looks a little awkward when she sees us but Alice carries on without missing a beat.

"Uhuh," says Alice, "but Mum says there's no way she's a

man. No 'man' could look that good without EXTENSIVE Botox."

"Can if you're beautiful already," says Laura, giving me a grin. She's catching on. I keep walking and say nothing cos I'm not sure what would come out. I don't even look up and I certainly do NOT hear the laughter that follows us. "Is this persecution?" says Laura. "Are we saints yet?"

"Getting there." She doesn't even insist on walking to class on her own. I think she understands that I need her a little bit today plus I'm worried that she might hear some of this stuff on her own.

~ ~ ~

I'm called to the school office before lunchtime. Laura's sitting on the plastic chair, swinging her legs back and forth.

"Is something wrong? Are you hurt?"

She shakes her head.

"Just turned up," says the school secretary, Mrs Morrissey. "I have let the junior school know she's here but she refused to leave without seeing you. Perhaps you could have a word with her. They're not meant to leave the school grounds during school time."

"I'll take her back now." I take Laura's hand and we head out. She doesn't say anything till we're outside.

"I didn't mean to get you into trouble." She sounds so little all of a sudden. "I was going to wait for you outside your classroom but you weren't there and then a teacher found me and brought me there."

"We move for different classes."

"Oh." She pulls her sleeves over her thumbs – she always puts holes there first. "She wasn't very happy."

"Never mind Mrs M. She was born grumpy. That's why her eyes are too close together, cos she frowned so much as a baby." At least this gets a smile. "Sure, you could be a secret messenger with a code for me to break." Her veil is askew though, so I know something has happened. "Want to tell me what this is about?"

I'm ready to jump on my High (Teenage) Horse and gallop down to the junior school to find out who upset my kid sister when she says, with big eyes looking up at me for the answer, "Why do people hate Dad?"

~ ~ ~

Turns out someone took photos of Dad – *Mandy* – at rugby practice on a phone and sent them to everyone. My tackle made it to YouTube and, granted, it is a mighty tackle but I can't take an ounce of pleasure in it because all anybody wants to do is whisper and point and snigger that Mandy's our dad. We don't have mobile phones – Dad's paranoid about screen-time and stalking – but someone helpfully showed the video and pics to Laura at little break before informing her that Dad is going to go to hell. The news spread through her disciples and whittled them down.

"Only evil people go to hell and Dad's the kindest person in the world, isn't he?"

She nods but I have a word with her teacher before she goes back into class and Laura is moved to sit beside the friend who defended her.

Then it's back into the maelstrom of lunchtime in my school. "Is it seriously the same person that attacked Mr D.?" This is in the corridor. "So he's what, changing into a woman?" By the lockers. "Weirdsville *Night of the Living Dead* stuff." "Yeah like *Welcome to Nightvale!*" Toilets. "Should he be let near kids?" Outside the staffroom. "D'you think they chop everything off?" Yard.

The last is from Alo's gang, a nest of zombie vipers all of them staring and whispering and some of them moving away as if I were contaminated. Surprisingly, it isn't Alo saying this; it's Rick, but I barely notice.

"Sure, my dad is transitioning into a woman." Enough, it seems, even for shy timid little me, is ENOUGH! As a tactic, it doesn't *exactly* stop the interest, but it brings it into the open. "Big deal." I turn to Rick. "You want to know how they turn a man into a woman? I mean, you thought Mandy was cool yesterday." He goes puce, from the ears up. Like a mood ring on a stove.

"Thing is, Rick, they use piranhas. To get rid of the boy bits. Their teeth are so sharp and so small, it makes for a clean cut and very little scarring." The boys wince. "Some people keep them as souvenirs. Door stops n stuff."

I'm not sure EXACTLY why but suddenly I'm unzipping my bag and pulling out all the leaflets and brochures. One by one, Alo's little court attaches itself to me, and then some of the girls too. "What about the breasts? Is it like Baywatch? Silicone n stuff?"

"They're lining up a new experimental drug to help them develop. He has to wear the right size bra so they'll know when to stop. If it works, he'll get a breast pump after the baby is born. When they start to lactate – that means give out milk – then the breasts start to grow naturally."

"That why your mum got pregnant?"

"Yeah, they're going to share the night feeds."

With Laura's little sad face before me, I fan the brochures out in front of their beady eyes. "Four euro each and they're yours to keep." While the supply lasts, I'm the centre of attention. Popular, even. But then everyone's gone and Abby's standing there with her arms crossed. I never saw her come up. She has 'that look' but I'm angry still.

"Why shouldn't I get something from it?!"

"You're turning him into a freak."

"No. I'm not. He's turning himself into a freak and I'm not going to let him! "

"You have no choice," she says, very quietly.

"Oh yeah?" says I. "Is that so?"

THIRTY FOUR

Mr D. is screaming into the phone when I walk straight past his secretary/minder/pet Doberman, Mrs Morrissey and into his office.

"What do you mean he did nothing wrong?! The man's a PERVERT! He came to my school! He stood in front of our pupils. He TALKED to them!" He waves Mrs M. away and points me to a chair. "Something's come up. I'll call you back." He bites aggressively into a chocolate digestive and the biscuit dies without a whimper.

I sink into the chair, watching the biscuit die. "You said you could help."

"Were the authorities to *realise* how badly your father's decision was affecting his children and their education…" He slides a leaflet across the table. The one about social workers. Intervention. Reporting families.

I push it back. "I can't."

"Of course. But if I were to… With your permission?"

This is all a terrible mistake and some other Jessie is standing here in this office listening and agreeing… You

218

know those times when you start something and even if you wanted to stop it, you wouldn't know how? I'm on an escalator going backwards at speed and I can't find my voice.

He takes my silence for a yes and holds out the biscuits.

"I'll get Jennifer to ring home and tell your parents you're staying overnight with us. Do your case no harm for you to show you prefer to stay with a normal family."

I think he's talking to himself but he's right. I can't go home tonight after coming here. There's too much stuff in my head and I'd end up saying something. "I need to bring Laura home first. Make sure Eva's there."

"Fine. Fine. Biscuit?"

"No. Thanks."

I'm being spat back into the real world when I find my voice. "They'll just tell him to stop, right?"

"You're doing this to save your family, and so am I," he says. "Remember that."

So why do I feel mussed up inside?

~ ~ ~

Abby is furious. "Why can't you just talk to him? *Her?*"

"Because *she's* my dad. And I tried that, remember?"

"You'd prefer to go into care."

"That's not what they do," I say, staring into the middle distance. "They'll make him stop. Your dad promised–"

"Yeah, cos he's your greatest fan!" she snorts, stalking ahead of me. "Why the hell do you think he would want to help you or your dad!?"

"What are you fighting about?" says Laura. Her last

disciple – there were three who didn't mind about Dad – has waved goodbye and now she's stuck with us. "Is it that boy?"

"No," we both say in unison.

"Is it Dad?"

~ ~ ~

I set Laura down with a toasted sandwich and her homework at the kitchen table and leave the room without looking back in case I blurt it out. Eva's in the living room cutting out reviews. She gives me a hug and says, "Enjoy yourself. I'm so happy for you to have a friend." Conflicted is *not* the word but I'm not ready to go there yet.

Abby's still not talking to me but that's okay. *I'm* not really talking to me. Alo's confused when he finds me putting my toothbrush in their bathroom. "What are you doing here?"

"It's a sleepover, Alo." Abby steers me into the safety of her room.

"Yeah and my right arm's a world class ballerina!"

I lie awake and tell myself I'm doing this for Laura, as well as Dad. I'm doing it for all of us.

So why does my tummy hurt?

Soon as Abby's asleep, I creep into Moodge's room. I know she won't mind. It's a cloudless night, full of stars and a little sickle moon. I nod the dogs' heads. I can see why she likes the nodding. There's a rhythm to it that blocks stuff out.

Nearly.

"Murderous sky," she says, from the depths of her bed. I

look to see if the sky has changed. "No shelter for poppies in that sky."

I never thought of clouds as poppy-shelters before but it works for me. Suddenly I know I've done something terrible; that poppies will die or be scattered and eaten by wolves because of me.

"Abby!" I shake her awake as if my life depends on it. I know she'll help because she's basically kind, unlike me. "I have to stop your dad from phoning them!"

She blinks to clear her head and slips on her glasses. "It's too late."

"If you spoke to him, told him I'd made a mistake? You could persuade anyone! He must be basically kind cos you're his daughter and even Alo hasn't said anything in school so maybe the genes are good there too despite, well, everything so your dad, he'll listen cos he loves you and–"

She interrupts me before I embarrass myself. "It's being fast-tracked. I overheard him tell Mum. He knows the Head of the Department."

So this is the end.

They'll take us away, put us in homes, give Dad electric shock treatment until he's normal again but he'll never be normal. I've read about it. He'll always forget he's eaten ice-cream and want to eat it again. Laura will hate me forever. Eva too.

"Look, it'll probably come to nothing." She's trying not to care but I know she does. That makes everything I've done ten times worse. "Who'd believe a raving lunatic like my dad anyway?" Funny, she doesn't sound convinced either.

"He's the Principal of a secondary school."

"True," she says, reluctantly. "So when they come you can tell them you made a mistake. Tell them the truth. *Warn your dad.*"

"Mandy."

"Yeah." Abby puzzles a bit. "You're right. It is weird." Then she pulls herself together, straightens up and looks me in the eyes. "Warn Mandy and he'll–"

My turn to interrupt. "*She*'ll–"

This time she ignores me. "Once Mandy knows what's going to happen, you can all put together a Plan of Action, a campaign."

That's when I get the brainwave. "I know! We'll simply show the social workers how happy we are!"

"Yeah."

Brilliant.

But will it be enough?

THIRTY FIVE

As I come in, Dad hangs up the phone and grins at me. "Seven thousand smackeroos! For one piece."

"Which one?"

"Field of Mammaries!" He gives me a hug, all warm and happy and proud. "Hell, if Eva's pieces keep selling like this, I'll never have to work again!"

"Maybe we could go live on a deserted island then." I'm with Laura there. It's as if he didn't even notice I wasn't here last night.

"Oh my little Laura; no deserted islands till we're all grown up. But speaking of money, a little birdie tells me one young lady was selling trade secrets for filthy lucre in the school yard yesterday." I shift foot, waiting for the explosion.

"Bet you scared the pants off the guys!" He grins like a cheetah. "I love the way you have snatched the lid off this thing at every opportunity."

Yeah, I'm brilliant. I don't feel brilliant. I feel a dusty shade of age old mud but at least I'm not in a red velour tracksuit.

"Nice time with 'The Family'?"

"They're just normal, Dad."

"Of course they are and for some people, that's absolutely perfect. As for us, in celebration of my wonderful girls, my new life and this latest sale… Oh and I shouldn't say anything yet but among Eva's guests were a number of people who might be in a position to commission some interesting buildings and that Eva is staying in town to be wined and dined by agents and collectors. Or that my crematorium may feature in the *Irish Times* next week! What? Didn't I mention that?!"

"No."

"Okay, well to mark all of this, the Keane ladies of leisure are going to have a film, popcorn, pizza, jello, the works. I think I even have a small packet of Tootsie Rolls hidden somewhere… Homework notes will be awarded to all!"

Suits me. The 'Family Crest' is due in tomorrow and I haven't exactly been in the mood to finish it.

~ ~ ~

Dad – Mandy – weeps copiously all the way through Bridget Jones' Diary. Again. "I bet we're related," he sniffs. I'm not sure whether to point out she's fictional. Again. Or just buy him the book for Christmas.

I don't get it how it's his favourite film. Bridget is not a great heroine. She's obsessed by weight, food, men and what underwear to wear. I guess him wanting to a woman doesn't mean he has to be a woman with good taste. When I look at him thinking this, I feel a pain in my stomach as if it's full of stale Tootsie Rolls and I have to remind myself, again, that I'm doing this for him, for Laura, the new baby, for all of us.

"I'm just so… happy," he says. "Me and my girls."

~ ~ ~

I lie awake and worry cos I don't know what words he will have used, what angry voodoo he might have invoked. In school, I keep my head down, avoiding conversations with The Exorcist, Nurse McCarthy, Mr D., Alo and everyone with whom I play rugby. On the Wednesday, there's a suspicious looking van parked near our house when we return from school so I make Laura walk on the other side of the road in case the social workers have decided to swoop. Two more days of vigilance and we're on our Easter holidays.

Eva's exhibition finishes up and the Gallery want to book her again next year. She now regards Mandy as her new good luck charm while Dad's already had a few tentative approaches from clients which is a sign to him that he's doing absolutely the right thing. Neither of them let us see the negative coverage or the sensational column inches in the tabloids but I'm sure they're there and I know one tabloid offered to pay for some of Dad's ops in return for a weekly diary but he said no.

The Darcy's head away for Easter. I miss seeing Abby but at least there's no chance of any run-ins between Mr D. and Dad. Eva takes Dad out shopping for new clothes too, which was a bit overdue and we all get subjected to a fashion parade and I begin to relax. Maybe all that happened was that they put note on a file saying, *Got call from raving loony. Action: ignore.*

Laura thinks I've gone barmy as I'm being really nice to her all the time.

~ ~ ~

First day back, we have the dreaded *Talk*. Girls first, in the Hall; boys after lunch. Lucky us. We get to hear *all about the changes your bodies are going to go through* and *respecting our own bodies and everyone else's…*

The Exorcist notices me fiddling and pulls me up in front of everyone to talk about, "How I feel about becoming a young woman".

"Can't wait," I say. "When I grow up I want to be a woman just like you." This gets a giggle from my audience that I acknowledge it with a bow and extra Spanish homework. Conjugating verbs to do with respect and behaviour.

"I don't know what has got into you or how you were allowed to behave in your last school Jessica Keane but that will not do here."

"Sorry, Ms O'Flaherty."

I bet she chose Spanish as her language because of her affinity to the conquistadors. It's probably KILLING her that she's limited to giving me detention or extra homework.

But I manage to keep my mouth shut on that one.

THIRTY SIX

Before I open the front door, I know I was foolish to relax. Eva, usually so careful not to pass bad vibes onto our future sib, is in the kitchen shouting at the top of her voice. "It's him," she says. "Of COURSE it's him!"

"Oh oh," says Laura and kneels down for a little prayer in the hallway. I don't mind. At least she didn't do it on the doorstep.

Eva's waving a letter at Dad. "It doesn't say that," he says, calmly. "It doesn't give any name or say we were reported by anyone. Maybe it's routine, given the circumstances. Maybe it was the hospital?" He gives me a wink, but I can see his heart's not in it and his cardigan is all askew. He still hasn't heard from Gaffa since the row and the school wrote to say they didn't need his assistance coaching the team. "How was school?"

"Forget school," says Eva. "We have to deal with this."

"What is it?"

I've never seen Eva so angry or Dad so worried. She passes me the letter.

Concerns have been raised... The letter is from the Department of Social Services. They want to visit Saturday afternoon. It could be an invitation to be decapitated at dawn by a grumpy Tudor king. My mouth goes dry.

"I'm right, amn't I, Jessie? It's that *gerbil* from next door, your friend's father." I manage a shrug. She turns to Dad. "You saw his face when he was leaving the exhibition!"

They're missing out on one important fact. "He's our Principal. You made him a laughing stock," I say, avoiding eye contact.

Well it's true. This isn't ALL my fault. If Dad hadn't been so shocked at the pinch, George wouldn't have stumbled. If Mrs D. hadn't let him drink two brandies before he left the house or if the Darcy's had only listened to me when I said it was a bad idea to go...

"So?" says Eva. "He is a laughing stock! He made a pass at your father!"

I didn't start this! "He made a pass at *Mandy*." There's a difference.

"You told them not to come?"

I avoid his eyes. "He'd been drinking. I thought he might spill wine on your crematorium." So I'm a liar, what's new? It's not as if I actually like myself right now anyway.

But Eva is not letting go. "Nobody asked him to lunge drunkenly at Mandy like a, like a–"

"It was more of a pinch," says Dad quietly. It doesn't help.

Eva takes my face in her hands, gently, so she can see into my eyes. Now I know how Laura's goldfish must have felt when they were dropped them into the tank with Ponchinello. I'm sure she can read my guilt but she strokes my cheek absently. "I know this is tough for you but I am right, amn't I? It's him!"

"Maybe."

Dad puts his arm around her. "I won't be dictated to, sweetheart. Not by anyone." He gives me a nod which says, let me sort this out and she'll be fine so I pick up my school bag and leave. "We've just got to prove that we are as normal a family as the next," he says as the door closes behind me.

Laura has dozed off with her head against the wall. I step over her little praying legs and think to myself, "Normal", as if THAT'S ever going to happen.

I have to make this stop.

~~~

I've barely put my finger on next door's bell when the door flies open as if he'd been expecting me. For a moment, I can't say anything. He's towering over me, framed by the door, Principal of my school. How could I have ever thought he'd spoken with a kind voice? I must have been delusional but that doesn't matter now.

I have to get through to him.

I can do this.

He listened before, right?

"Tell them you made a mistake." My voice cracks. It always lets me down. "Please." He doesn't even blink. I have this feeling that for him I'm merely an earwig messing up his tidy lawn. "It's nothing to do with you."

229

BIG mistake.

He brandishes the *Weekly Hound* newspaper in my face. Now I know the difference between anger and wrath. Wrath, it's a very *angry* anger, the sort of anger that would sit in a blazing fire filing its nails and not even feel the heat. 'Principal at Transsexual Party' reads the headline. 'Closet Homosexual attacks Lesbian Artist?'

This just goes to show how wrong the papers can be.

"This!" he hisses, "is HIS idea of fun. Your *'father's'* idea" – and here he nearly spits – "of *neighbourliness!*?" I've unleashed a monster.

"It's a rubbish paper. Nobody reads it. They make it all up! Everyone knows that. You could sue. You could write to them? *I* could write?"

"Nobody messes with George P. Darcy and gets away with it." He straightens up as if he expects a halo to come down and anoint him. "The world will see him for the pervert he is and they'll take him away. Oh yes! You and your sister will go into care, learn decent values, forget all you've ever known. And we, *we* will return" – he takes a deep breath and his face seems to relax from the top down – "to *normal.*"

I've never hated this word so much as I do when he says it.

He scans the estate as if it belonged to him. As if every blade of grass that isn't of uniform length is a personal affront. "Believe me," he adds, cheery as an egg. "It's for the best."

Then he steps back and closes the door very quietly.

I can't move an inch. I know that tomorrow, he will walk through the school with a new spring in his step. He'll lecture us on justice at Assembly and taking action for the good of all. He'll send out for fresh supplies of chocolate digestives and bite into them with so much satisfaction that half of every biscuit will end up in the carpet but he won't even notice.

A good day to be a termite, if Ireland had termites and they lived in overheated offices.

Abby slips out the side passage to see if I'm okay. She heard my voice at the door but she didn't hear what he said cos he speaks really low when he's mad and that's what got her worried.

"You could still talk to him, Abby. He'd have to listen to you?"

"Since when?" She fishes out a piece of cake from her pocket and gives me half. "You should have told him – *her* – your dad how you felt in the first place."

No. That's not fair. She's my friend. She should be supporting me and sympathising and telling me she'll help. "Ever get tired of being right?"

"What?"

"No. Course not cos you're always right. It's as if you have some monopoly on 'right'. Like you were born being right. You probably don't even have a left foot or a left hand because that would suggest you could be something other than right!"

"That's not fair."

"Some of us. Don't. Have. That. Okay?"

THIRTY SEVEN

"I can't believe you managed to fit us in so quickly," says Eva. Dad brings in a pot of tea and the nice biscuits Eva has hidden all week from him so they'd be here now. He's in a gun-green blouse and trousers. It's not his best look but it's okay. "Isn't this fantastic, Mandy? I only wrote to them last week!"

She's brilliant. Her pre-emptive strike completely floors the social worker with the file who checks through the paperwork to find reference to her approach. He has a lugubrious face, like a very sad frog. "You contacted us?"

Eva versus the Social Workers; Eva – one; social workers – nil.

His colleague looks more sceptical. She probably did drama lessons as a child or maybe the job makes you suspicious of everyone which is understandable. Parents can be terribly good liars when it comes to their children.

"Oh yes." Eva sits down opposite him as if this was a meeting she had been actively looking forward to. "About counselling for the girls."

"Really? We don't seem to have any record of your request." He looks at his colleague who shakes her head.

Eva's on a roll. She will bewilder them with enthusiasm. It works in all the Spanish *Novellas* we've watched for years but it might be a first for these guys. "Obviously, we are all supportive of Mandy's decision…" Hand squeeze for Dad. "But we do worry that we might miss something. So we thought, the girls might talk freely – more freely, the way a cat will play with a ball in a room where there are no dogs – with trained counsellors, with professionals like yourselves…"

Yeah, like I talked to Mr D. *That* went REALLY well.

"…About concerns they would not tell their parents…"

"Sounds like a good decision," he says and writes something down.

"Though of course we would hope Jessie and Laura can talk to us about anything, as I imagine most parents do."

All I can think of is how do we get out of this without it going really, really bad and it then being always and ever MY fault that Laura lost her parents and Eva's baby had to grow up without siblings.

(I'd probably end up breaking out of care and finding Laura so we could run away but maybe we wouldn't be able to survive in the wild and she would get sick so I'd end up in Juvie sharing with some girl who juggles knives, but what would be worse would be knowing I had destroyed our family.)

"A lot of people in your situation would feel threatened."

He smiles at me. It must be a tricky job, being always unwelcome. Or mostly. By some family member's at least.

Having to be careful not to make a mistake cos lives could be at risk. My head's so full of Negative Thoughts that I forget to smile back. Then I think I *should* have smiled cos now he'll think there is something on my mind – and there is, but it's not what he thinks – but then this noise breaks through and everyone jumps.

Mr Darcy is strimming his already trim front garden, trying to see in the front window, I'd worry for his toes. Nobody bats an eyelid, not even the female social worker who must be wearing false eyelashes cos they're getting tangled in her fringe. Dad – *Mandy* – picks up the teapot that must be halfway cold and says, "Tea?"

As if this is all a game in which hostilities must cease for refreshments.

As if we're *not* being spied upon by our neighbour.

"Actually, no," she says. You can tell she doesn't believe in fraternising with the natives at this stage. "We'd like to talk to talk to each of your children individually, after having a little talk with the two of you."

"I'll get the sugar." I dive into the kitchen as if they'd all said they wanted tea *desperately,* were *dying* of the thirst and forgetting why they'd really come to our house. Eva follows and I tell her about Mr D. She suggests to the social workers that the kitchen might be a more comfortable place to talk.

~ ~ ~

First off, they ask Eva and Dad about the baby, how life was in L.A. and do they have people to vouch for them as parents? People in authority? Laura and I listen at the door until Laura decides that praying will help. I persuade her to do it upstairs. The questions go on and on. How would they describe a normal day and have they noticed anything different with our behaviour?

"Such as?" says Dad but they're not feeding info here, only gathering. Do we talk a lot and if so, which of us talks most? Oh and what would they regard as normal punishment, what would be our bedtime routine and why did they think someone might have suggested there was a problem?? Eva says some people probably feel uncomfortable with Dad's decision but that says more about them. So then they ask does Dad think his decision is fair to us? How had he introduced the subject, how much will we be told and how does he think it will change things for us? And, of course, he oozes pride at our support.

Then they move into the living room and it's Laura's turn. I warn her NOT to mention the grave and sneak upstairs to make a call from Dad's office.

"Gramma? They're going to take us away!" I only meant to say, *'Maybe you should come round* or *It might be a good idea if you called over'*. Instead, I have Gramma trying to calm me down while to explain what's happening and that maybe, if they came over too, they could tell these people that we were fine.

That we ARE fine.

When Laura comes to fetch me from our room, I ask her what she told them, in case there's something I have to fix. She says she doesn't remember and I know she wouldn't say anything knowingly bad.

That's more likely to be me and I'm up next.

~ ~ ~

"It's my fault you're here. I got into a fight at school and the Principal, Mr Darcy, he thought it must be cos of what was happening at home. But it's not. It's because he fancies Mandy. He's been peeping over the wall and everything."

Well? This is *WAR!* But I don't know why I bother. In the same way Dad never notices it when I stomp upstairs, they don't seem to listen to anything I've said; as if I was making stuff up!

As if I'd need to!

"Our source said that Laura was 'digging a grave'?"

"She wants to be a saint. It's not so odd." Okay, it is but I'm not saying that to them. Normal, normal, we are UTTERLY normal. Just a bit quirky. Right? "She wants to be really special is all. Probably cos she has nuns teaching her now or ex-nuns and that scary crucifix in the classroom. I mean, why would you put something like that up in a classroom, a sculpture of a man being tortured to death?"

I take a moment to let this sink in, making sure they understand.

"Anyway, she got it into her head that she should try being dead and resurrected to see what it would feel like to be a saint. But not for real. And it's nothing to do with Dad. Laura's always been into religion n stuff. Some kids collect stickers; Laura collects The Lives of Saints."

"So the visions she mentioned?" The woman social worker refills her glass of water at the sink. I remember her name now. Alice. Figures; she has long hair. If it wasn't tied back, it'd probably be flicky too.

Okay, I can't say Laura saw Dad in a dress and thought he was the Virgin Mary because I'm not sure if it should be in the public record. "She's very imaginative…. Didn't wash her foot for weeks after Daniel Radcliffe visited our school and stepped on it by mistake."

A muddy face appears at the window, Alice screams and everything I've said is forgotten. The other social worker, whose name is Fred – I know cos she screams it really loudly – , heads outside as Eva and Dad spill in and then we are all joined by a very dishevelled and muddy Mr Darcy followed by Fred.

"I fell in a grave. A grave!"

"This is our neighbour, George Darcy," says Eva. "He prunes his trees at night so he can spy on us." So she did notice! The look Fred and Alice exchange confirms for Eva that it *was* Mr D. who reported us.

"At night, don't be ridiculous! However, I *was* pruning my plum tree just now when the branch snapped, firing me over the wall into that child's grave!" He points a long finger at Laura who steps behind me.

I can see by Eva's face that she's all for putting a Paddington Bear sign on Mr D. and depositing him on the doorstep next door but Dad says, "Maybe it's time you went home now, George." When he puts a hand on Mr D.'s elbow to guide him out, the man jumps, backs into the hall and out the door as Gaffa's panther purrs into the driveway.

Gaffa can't look Dad quite in the eye but he doesn't want to show weakness so he heads straight into the kitchen as if

Gramma were sweeping him forward with a Broom of Immense Strength. Looking at no-one in particular, he growls, "Tea'd be nice". Gramma gives Dad the biggest hug, fixes the line of his cardigan to hang better and says, "Come on then". They follow Gaffa in and the 'hellos' begin.

Gramma pulls a t-shirt out of the box Gaffa's carrying and hands it to Laura, then another for me and Eva. "Research suggests that it helps to be upfront and open about this whole thing right from the beginning. So, I thought, why not proclaim, '*My Son's a Woman*'!"

Except it doesn't.

It says, 'My Best Friend's an Anchovy.'

Nobody says anything at first. Gramma smiles as if we were all a bit dim. "It's street code. Anchovies, they change sex too. Apparently."

Fred says he thinks it's only certain crabs that change but not anchovies since they're only fish. "What's wrong with fish?" says Laura, leading to a defence of predatory fish such as Ponchinello and how we are all fish really since we came from the sea. Amid the discussion, the day's work somehow finishes for the team. Questionnaires are packed away and cups of tea are brewed. They'll keep in touch but it seems Mr D. showing up in the guise of a muddy stalker has considerably helped our case. Oh how that will freak it him out!

Alice-as-in-rabbits leans in to Gaffa. "You really don't mind?"

Gaffa clears his throat. "It's not easy. I can't say it's easy – he's my only son! – but I'm sure he… *she* hasn't made this decision lightly." Dad's eyes fill up when he hears this and there's this awkward hug. "I was a stripper, you know," Gaffa says, pulling away and lifting his chin in the air.

"Did a right wicked FBI chief," says Gramma.

Okay, I get it. This is them getting rid of the social workers. It's all an act. "What's a stripper?" says Laura as the doorbell rings again and I think *who now?*

THIRTY EIGHT

Half expecting to see Mr D. with an axe when I open the door, I find Abby instead. With a cake.

"Hey."

."Hey."

"Come in, come in," Gramma shouts out. "More the merrier!"

Abby merges right in, like a benign sea anemone. Her Mum sent her in to apologise. "She says he needs a holiday. Everything he's done, including writing to you, it came from the stress and he's going to write an official apology." She winks at me behind their backs as if to say, '*Mum will write the letter. Dad will sign cos he's tired of sleeping on a pull-out bed*'.

Far from patching things over so that we won't get taken into care, the kitchen is now buzzing. Cups are exchanged for glasses of Prosecco – also brought by Gramma – as if there were something to celebrate, though the social workers stick with tea. Everyone, says Eva, has so much to talk about and so much to learn.

~ ~ ~

I have one photo of my original family with all of us in it. I'm six, piggybacking with my arms around Dad's neck. When I was littler, I'd hold his ears, he said; pretend he was a horse. Mum's linking his arm and smiling at the camera.

She has the smallest bump under her dress and that bump's Laura.

If you look closely, maybe you can see that she's not well. But you can't see that she has cancer and doesn't know it yet. You can't see that the baby she's carrying is masking her cancer so nobody will know until it's too late or that she'll say no to chemo because of that baby and we'll be all alone.

"Mandy said you'd be here."

I slip the photo into my pocket as Abby steps out onto the Cloud Platform. "I'm sorry about the other day."

"'S'okay." Abby slides down beside me. "Told you it'd be fine. Mandy could talk newborn babies into walking." She stares into the sky. "So have you ever, y'know?"

"Ever what?"

"Wanted to be, I dunno, Joan of Arc or something?"

"It doesn't run in families, Dad's thing. It's not genetic. It's just him. *Her*."

"But can't you understand why she does it?! I mean, you must have wanted to be different. Jeez, I used to wish I'd been swopped at birth and my real mum ran a chocolate shop! Can you imagine!?"

I want to pierce her good mood with a spear. "My sister wants to be a saint though she's only been inside a church

241

twice. My stepmother makes sexy statues I can't even show anyone. My dad's calling himself Mandy and is considering liposuction in reverse to give *himself* hips."

I take a deep breath and touch the photo in my pocket. My body aches all over and when I answer, my voice feels far away and lost. "No, Abby. All I ever wanted was to be the same as everyone else.

She doesn't say anything for the longest time. A skinny whale cloud evaporates into flotsam above us. Right, now's the time they decide to throw shapes I can see.

"Least they're not boring."

~ ~ ~

Fred and Alice leave at five, promising to organise family counselling and to launch an enquiry into Mr D.'s complaint. There's mention of a family holiday, back in time to a simpler place, but maybe that was wishful thinking.

I didn't want them to split us up but surely, SURELY someone can see that this is wrong. Dad is Dad. He's not Mandy or Lou-Lou or Fifi Fluffy Flower Petal. I keep waiting for someone to say this or hint at it or even to ask the question but NOBODY does.

Next thing I know, I'm shovelling soil into Laura's grave. Dad should never have let her dig a STUPID grave. Same way he should have stopped her wearing a veil and saying she wanted to be a nun and a saint and kneeling down in the hallway. I've seen how Abby prays and it's not the same as what Laura does. Her praying is formal and there are proper starts and finishes and you kneel by your BED and

NOBODY taught us how and Mum isn't here so she never got a chance to tell us anything and everything's all, all UTTERLY wrong.

All I can do to make it better is shovel lumpy dirt into a sticky hole and get rid of the one thing that's so obviously wrong.

"Want to tell me what's up?" I didn't even hear him coming. He puts his hand on my arm to stop me shovelling. "Jessie?" But I'm not stopping. I'm NOT stopping till the whole horrible grave has disappeared.

"How the hell am I meant to make friends when my sister dresses like a freaky nun and digs her own grave?"

"Think of the fun you'll have reminding her about it when she's older."

And that is just IT. That's it!

"I didn't sell those brochures because I was proud of you. I wanted people to see you for the freak you are." I throw the shovel on the ground.

"No, love. You wouldn't do that."

"I'm sick of it. Sick of smiling and pretending everything's alright. Yeah, we're just the average, normal happy family."

He grabs my arm as I pass. "Why didn't you tell me?"

I pull away. "Right! That would have worked! *Oh Jessie understands, don't you love?* That made it so much easier! *At least we're honest with you...* All girls together... We don't want you excluded!

I barely take time to breathe. Now I've started, it all has to come out or I'll explode into tiny stinky pieces and we might as well have kept the grave to bury the bits in. "How about I didn't WANT to know everything? How about I DON'T want to know about your stupid operations and your implants and how beautiful you're going to be? And having to be REAL careful in case I say something wrong and then you go and hurt yourself."

He doesn't say a word.

"Mr Darcy didn't make me tell him ANYTHING. I went to him! I wanted them to take you away cos you're sick and you need help and you're not my dad! Not anymore."

Then I walk away.

I walk right away and I don't look back.

~ ~ ~

The Cloud Platform isn't far enough away from everyone right now so I keep going up until I'm up on the roof. The tiles are easy to climb, if you don't look down. I've never been so high but I'm not afraid of anything anymore.

I can hear them calling me and I don't care. They can point and stare and panic but none of it matters. I'm back in L.A. All alone and safe; nothing matters and nothing has changed.

One cloud hides in the sky. It's not very big and it's not very brave but if I ask it to, that cloud will swoop down and carry me off and keep me far away from everything. I only have to think of the right words to lure it down.

Dad appears beside me on the roof and first I think, *Why has he followed me here? Why can't he leave me ALONE?* But when I look across, he's sweating and white and I know he could fall. But it's NOT MY FAULT. I didn't ask him to follow me here. I came up so no-one would follow me.

So nobody could.

"I don't want to grow up, Dad. I don't like your world. I don't like the way it gets all mixed up and everything's hard to understand. I just want to be normal."

It starts to rain. I turn my face up to it; it feels so cool and lovely on my face. "I don't remember her, Dad."

I'm not afraid, not really, of words anymore.

"I don't remember what Mum looked like or how she smelt or if her hair was really golden or if she dyed it and how her hugs felt or if she was scared of heights too or flying…And now I'm losing my dad too."

"Jessie, I–"

Something in his voice makes me turn. I see this pain in his eyes. It's a reflection of mine only his pain is for me, not for himself. And I think, *I can't do this anymore*. I have to make it right so I am moving back towards him because I want him to hold me and tell me it will all be alright and I want to believe him.

Only a tile slips.

A silly little tile.

I can see his hand, the fingers, the nails that need a manicure, they're inches from mine and I'm gone.

"JESSIE!"

I never knew I could fly.

THIRTY NINE

"She's conscious!"

Drips and fruit and balloons. Dad kisses me on the forehead. "It's okay, love. It's okay." So the cloud caught me. It skimmed the sky, wrapped me in jello and put me to bed. Eva's there smiling at me from the end of the bed.

Nurses appear and ask me questions. *Do you know what day it is?* Dad's mascara is smudged; my panda-dad. *Your name? Date of birth?* There is a fly on the ceiling. I think it might be Michael Jackson. *Address? Phone number?* I know the answers to them all, 'specially the last. "I don't have one. Dad won't let us have mobile phones."

He smiles. I reach up to wipe his mascara away but nothing happens and all I hear is, "Hey!" really softly, as if he's crying inside and then Eva's hugging him and everything goes dark.

When I wake up again, the balloons are gone. Dad's still there, his eyes de-pandified.

"Your arm is fractured. That's why you can't move it and you broke a leg, but it's a clean break." He plays with the fingers of my good hand. "You were really lucky, love. You landed on a bush, so your back and neck are fine and so's your head. Your daft, lovely head."

I know what he's saying. "Dad—"

"Hush."

It could have been so much worse. I feel so STUPID and SELFISH and…

"It's okay. I'm glad you told me."

"Really?"

"But next time, choose somewhere closer to the ground. I mean, most stroppy teens go to their bedrooms and slam the door but not MY Jessie. She has to turn into a steeplejack—"

"Steeple-Jessie."

It's Laura; she has become witty. She has no veil, which looks odd. The crown of her head is totally round.

"A *right* Jessie," I say, like Gramma.

Dad said I talked a lot while I was 'out'. They got rid of the balloons when I got upset that they could fly and I couldn't. "Actually you said you couldn't fly because you weren't Michael Jackson. And what's with the jello?"

It comes back in fragments like an uncooked Chinese meal. First some gurgling, a feeling of nausea, a noodle or a bit of spring roll… It's as if I was frozen until I fell, but now I'm full of bits of broken ice.

When it thaws, I'll be alright.

"I never meant to hurt you, love," says my big beautiful Dad. "I'll make it better. Whatever it takes."

"I filled in the grave properly," says Laura. "Alo says he'll help me plant a tree in it. "

~ ~ ~

"Abby, he's ancient."

"Yeah but seriously, have you ever seen a cuter doctor!? Maybe he has a son?" She picks at my bed cover. "What were you doing? Pretending to be a bird?"

"I am a *bird*."

"Eagle then."

"Maybe I was a cloud."

"Pretty heavy one. You came down fast enough."

~ ~ ~

"About your mum–" says Dad. "We'll talk more."

"Wouldn't take much to be *more*."

"Okay, I deserve that. I thought we could put together an album, you and I, with stories alongside so you have all my memories too. You were right. Laura should hear us talking about her Mum more. I shouldn't have left it all up to you.

"As for the other thing…"

~ ~ ~

Abby says: "Don't you dare do anything so immensely stupid again." I nod. She holds out a baby finger. "Pinky swear."

I don't do pinky swears cos they're lame and for littlies but I do it now. "Pinky swear."

"So, the doctor…. Have you asked?"

"No."

"But this is the BEST opportunity! If he has a son, then you say you're lonely and feeling awful and he persuades his son to come into work with him next time and love blossoms…"

"You read too many books."

"Least people don't jump off roofs in books."

"Sure they do and I didn't jump." I open up the box of chocolates Gaffa sent in. Abby loves chocolates but they never have them at home. I wait till she's half way through the first layer before I add, "Besides, a cloud was meant to catch me."

"Just promise me. If you do say something and he has a son and if– a *cloud*?"

"I'll hobble to a phone and ring you if he has a son."

"You'd better. And to be clear, clouds aren't that strong. If you'd listened at Geography, you'd know they're are full of hot air. Except the wet ones and sure they're too busy dissolving to catch a flying dork like you so don't do it again."

"I won't. How's your dad?" I say to change the subject.

She shrugs. Mr D. was seriously scared when he heard about the accident cos, Abby says, he felt it was his fault. "He locked himself in the attic for hours. Alo couldn't even do his homework, that's how bad Dad was. When he came out, he'd been crying; kept asking Mum how had he turned into *this horrible person*."

They all went for a long, LONG walk – I can imagine Alo LOVING that – until they got good and lost. Seems my accident has made everyone think that it isn't important what people do or who they are, so long as they don't hurt each other or die. "Mum did a big picnic and we each had to say what bothered us."

He's resigning from his job as Principal and going back to teaching Maths, which is what he really loves. Turns out ten years ago he rescued two kids from a family where bad things happened. This was why the social welfare people responded so fast when he rang. It makes me feel a bit better towards him.

He *meant* to be kind but got it wrong.

"Mum says he only became Principal because he felt time was running out to make his mark. He's writing poetry again. Turns out lots of maths teachers are poets or singers; something to do with metres and stuff…" She stops short. I've a feeling there is more to say but she's not ready and that's fine. We have the rest of our lives to find out everything about each other, cos that's what best friends do.

"He'll be okay."

"Yeah."

She produces a sherbet dip. "Alo sent you this. He was talking to Laura for ages over the wall and then he gave me this to bring in. Don't ask why." Thank you, Laura. "Maybe he fancies you?"

"Yuk."

"Hey, we could be sisters-in-law. I could be your bridesmaid."

"Ouch. Don't make me laugh, it hurts." A pigeon lands on the windowsill and observes us with a steel-rimmed eye.

"Is it true you broke a rib?"

"Bruised. FEELS broken."

"Hey! That's what your dad should do," says Abby. "Like, if he was religious, he could get his rib taken out and then put back in and he wouldn't be a man anymore."

~~~

Gramma brought me a cloud book and a diary. "In case you want to write stuff down you don't want any of us to see. It has a lock and all." I'm about six years beyond locked diaries but I thank her with all my heart because I know I scared her and I'm sorry for it. Gaffa kisses my forehead and says nothing in case he cries.

Alo turns up the following day, all on his ownsome with a BOX of sherbet dips. "Dad asked what you'd like and I said–" He looks pretty sheepish so I let him sit down though I've no idea what we'll talk about.

"I think we've half-stolen your cat," he says. "Mum thought she was a stray. I told Mum tos top feeding her and your dad–" He corrects himself. "*Mandy* to buy nicer cat food to get her back for you."

I say thanks and offer him a dip. He's actually quite good at filling me in on all the gossip at school. Professional counsellors came in to talk to Year 2 after what happened, which is mortifying. Alo says everyone was chuffed cos it meant they got off Religion and The Exorcist has her nose out of joint cos she thinks she could have handled it perfectly well.

He talks about how much he loves photography. "But not like the paparazzi. I want to make people see things in a different way, y'know." He smiles, sort of embarrassed. "Get under the surface of stuff."

He has quite a nice smile, surprisingly.

FORTY

Before I can go home there are tests. Psychiatric tests. Personality tests. A priest asks if I am depressed and a counsellor wants me to play with a sandpit. It takes me a while to realise they seem to think I did this on purpose.

That's when I find my voice. "No. Really, I didn't want– I DON'T want to die. The fall was an accident. I was moving over to Dad so we could go back down. And yes, I was hurting inside but we've sorted it."

Dad's been interviewed too and Eva, and the social workers.

~ ~ ~

"You're coming home!" Laura bursts in ahead of Eva as if this is the best and only thing that's important to her. I ask her how it feels not to wear the veil.

"Draughty."

Minutes later Dad follows them in, having parked the car. He's all shaven and brushed and smelling of aftershave. That's when I know what he told the hospital and why they've let me go home.

"Well," he says, ever so quietly. "What d'you think?"

I don't say anything for a minute and then I smile. "*Suits you.*" We hug, but not too tight cos my ribs still feel as if they were danced upon by buffalo.

"Why don't you take Jessie out front," says Eva, "while we pack up her things?"

He wheels me down through the corridors, past people waiting for visits and patients in hospital gowns trying to get well by walking a few steps here and there. There's a woman crying, crying into her hands as if no-one will see because she's hiding the tears in her hands. There's a man trying to calm a small child who doesn't want to be here. DOESN'T DOESN'T DOESNT. Out past the newsagents and the bakery and the reception, down the ramp into the sunshine.

I think Dad would keep going. He'd walk and walk as far as he could only we have to stop and wait for the others. It has to be just us for a little while and I don't know where to start. Knowing what he's done, for me, I don't know what to say or how to be easy with him.

If I can make it like the old days, it'll be okay so I point at the sky with my good arm. "A tiger having puppies!"

"Sorry, love?" He tries to focus where I'm pointing.

I try again, though my heart isn't in it. "Ah no, it's Gramma's hair," which is silly cos it really isn't.

Dad squints up with his hand over his eyes. "That's right. Very good. Gramma."

I'm suddenly so tired. "I love you Dad."

"I know love."

And he does, but he sounds soft and sad, like a little fluffy white cloud about to fly into a windmill. He strokes my hand, gently. "Here they come!" Springing to his feet, he waves at Eva and Laura. Only then he seems surprised to find himself wearing a suit and tries to straighten invisible creases in the arms and legs.

"It'll be alright Dad," I say, but he doesn't hear.

~ ~ ~

A *Welcome Home* banner straddles the chimney breast. I recognise Laura's touch: it's written in letters made up of little golden fish. "I didn't put Ponchinello on it cos I know you never liked him," she says and hugs me tight.

"Ouch!"

~ ~ ~

"Let me guess. Chicken Kiev or sausage n chips?"

Eva decided we should celebrate my recovery the following weekend as a family. It has been an odd week. Everyone getting used to Dad being Dad and no-one else while trying not to talk about anything at all and school has been weird. People staring and treating me like I might break if they say boo. The first time in my life when I would love to be buried alive in homework and everyone takes it easy on me. I can even go home if I'm feeling tired or lie down in sickbay for a bit. Like I said, weird.

I picked the restaurant in Gramma's favourite store so Dad could have a whole sticky bun to himself. Gramma and Gaffa come too. There are pictures of families on all the ads around the cafe, which is a bit spooky.

Gramma talks on and on about how the store has changed and keeps squeezing my hand, but Gaffa is quiet as an empty house. I try to catch his eye but it's as if looking at me makes him remember how bad things nearly were.

Dad's growing a moustache. Slowly. It's like a slug sprayed with Grow-Your-Own that is desperate to escape. Eva's in a filmy maxi dress that makes her look like she and the baby could float away, but she's not smiling much. "It's the baby. Kicking so much now."

It never kicks for me so I talk to the baby in my head and explain that I did this so he or she would have a *real* Dad.

~ ~ ~

"So, a dog? What do you think Jessie?"

"Why can't we get an anteater?" says Laura.

"Because we don't know how anteaters are around babies," says Dad.

"Like that's the only reason."

"That's enough," says Gramma.

"What do you mean by that?"

Laura pushes the food around her plate. "Jessie doesn't like anteaters."

"I have no opinion. Really."

"Okay so you hate all animals?"

"I don't."

"That's enough love," says Eva, to Laura, "eat some more".

"Saints don't eat spinach."

"Just eat," says Dad, a bit too loud. "We're a happy

family having a nice normal family outing."

Nobody looks up, except me.

This is not how I imagined it. Everyone playing roles in some creepy film nobody ever wanted to see. "I need to pee." Dad says he'll come with me, in case, well, just in case and I don't bother saying, "It's okay, I won't fall" because he's already on his feet.

~ ~ ~

The toilets are at the back of the store, past all the lovely evening dresses Dad was looking at back in March. I stare in the mirror for ages. "This is what I wanted. This is what I wanted," I say, over and over. "This is normal."

But I have to come out eventually.

When I do, I'm still saying it in my head and there's Dad looking at this green dress. It's an action replay. Over to the right, Alice, Megan are browsing, with their mothers this time, in almost exactly in the same place they were when Dad and I were last here. Only this time, it's different. Cos I make a choice. Right there.

And for the first time in ages it feels like the RIGHT one.

"It's not your colour."

But Dad doesn't get it. He doesn't HEAR what I'm saying. He shoves the dress back onto the rail with an, "I'm sorry. It wasn't, I wasn't—"

I launch myself over to the next rack and pull out the silky red dress he looked at the last time. It's not his size but I hold it up against him so we can see how it might look. *"This* is MUCH more you."

"B-but–"

This time, I'm not making any more mistakes. "You need new shoes too. 'Specially for this dress." I swing past the girls with him following me and as we pass, I say, "Hi Megan, Alice".

Normal as can be.

"This is my dad. She's a woman in a man's body but we're going to change all that, aren't we Dad? "

He takes me aside. "You don't have to do this love."

"I want to." The girls are still there. "Love to chat but I'm kind of busy. Dad needs all the help she can get right now. We have to discuss what happens next; breast sizes, you know. She wants Double D but that's way too big."

"We what?"

And, simple as that, Dad is out.

My dad, Mandy.

Extract from the sequel to
Dad's Red Dress...

I'm back up at the top of the class again, only this time everyone's waiting. Really quietly. Now I know what Laura's (now dead) goldfish felt when they were put in the tank with Ponchinello. It's a sea of eyes, watching and waiting to see if I'm food. Abby gives me a grin and a thumbs up.

This is it then. This is me putting it all out there so there's no more whispering or pointing or making fun of me or Laura or Dad. Showing we're proud of her. Yes. *Her.* It's not as bad as the first day. I haven't knocked over the Principal or spilt coffee on Ms O'Flaherty who is standing beside me looking totally proud of herself. She's feeling liberal now. All her issues with my behaviour have been explained by my abnormal family but, being liberal – she thinks – means she is open and accepting and thinks it's a fantastic idea for me to make a little personal announcement.

Little? Not really. Personal? Absolutely. But where do I start? I don't even know what they know already, though I'm sure Megan and Alice got the word out. Who would have thought it'd be Megan who saves me by asking the easiest question?

"How'd he tell you?"

Before I can answer, Alice chimes in with what half the class are probably thinking: "Did you, like, find him in your underwear?!"

Now I'm on track. Hackles up, but calm and collected. "My dad's not a pervert, Alice. She's trapped in the wrong body. Same way you think you're smart but you're not and you think everyone likes you." This got a giggle from most of the class, but not in a mean way. Even she seemed to like the comeback.

Having been the worm, I have TURNED. I have teeth and am fearless (mostly). Which shows that if you're not afraid of the truth, it stops being a secret people can slag you about because you stop being afraid it'll come out.

"So how *did* he tell you?" says Megan.

I take a deep breath and I bring them with me to the hillside near the house we lived in six years ago. "We were watching clouds and he says, *'I'm not like other dads'*, which seemed a bit obvious.

"So I said, *'I know,'* thinking he was messing about. *'You're special!'*

"And he said, 'No. I mean really,' and pointed up at the sky. 'Know how you like to find a cloud and let it lift you up onto it? You float around a fluffy seagull called Florence, leaving your worries down here for the worms? You've told me, it feels as if you're completely yourself and everything's possible and… In those clouds, I'm a woman, Jessie, not a man.

"'It's the way I am.'"

Everyone is sitting really still. Some of them look at me as if it was a beautiful story and they will never see clouds in the same way. Ms O'Flaherty starts a discussion about how many of us want to be something we aren't and how much does how we *look* affect how we *act*…

It's as if they've forgotten my dad's becoming a woman and really, it's not even that interesting anymore.

Alo even smiles at me.

What I don't tell them is that the night before Dad told me, I'd seen an enormous cloud shaped like a stiletto. There was a sunset so it was dyed all sorts of shades of red and pink and gold. Because I'd seen that stiletto the night before Dad told me she was a woman inside, well *that's* why I started watching clouds REALLY closely every after.

If you have patience, they can be really helpful at preparing you for stuff to come.

~ ~ ~

Dad put purple and red stripes on my crutches so they would be more like a fashion accessory than a necessity. I can fly about on them so fast now I think I might miss them when they go. Abby's nicknamed me the Eagle.

"More like *Ostrich*," says Alo when he has an audience, but he opens doors for me and even carried my bag to school once. It's hard to manage on crutches. He means that I tried to fly but couldn't... but the trouble with being an ostrich is that sand can mummify your brain and make you do stupid things and hate yourself.

He walks home with us now, sometimes. Maybe he doesn't need to be so tough when his dad's not Principal. Even says interesting stuff, like and how some crustacean starts life being blue but turns pink or that the Mynah Bird can imitate anything, even a lawnmower or a forest fire.

He says his dad's buying him a hamster if he continues getting good marks and he wants to call it Widget.

~ ~ ~

Turns out nobody likes Dad's new name except Dad and even she has admitted it's a bit girly. *Frances* is Gramma's choice, maybe because it could sound male or female and that might make it easier for Gaffa to use. Laura wanted *Bridget,* so they could be saints together. I said people would think Dad had chosen it because of her favourite film and vetoed it.

And yes, the veil is back but she takes it off going to school.

I suggested *Amanda* because I've never known anyone called Amanda who got picked upon or bullied and it's close enough to Mandy for Dad to get used to it. Eva suggested *Dawn* or *Pixie* (yeah, weird). Dad finally chose *Amanda,* which was great until she added, "Cos it has all my identities in it: *a man, Da!* Get it?! and *Amanda!"*

Hold the loo lid up while I barf entire whales.

I must remember to think things through before I make a suggestion EVER again.

Laura's telling everyone that Ponchinello was the first in the family – yeah, in the 'family' – to transition into a girl. "He was a boy fish," she explains. Forgetting to mention a boy fish *that ate all the other fish* and even his own young. "Then he had babies and became a girl."

"Then he died," says I.

When I get a chance.

~ ~ ~

"Don't do that."

"Didn't." She does it again. "Laura, I'm warning you!"

"What's wrong? It's only cotton wool. 'Snot going to break."

"It's a cloud and it's only sellotaped on till I know where it's going to go so it's very delicate." I've finally finished the model of our house in L.A. This is the finishing touch – working out where to hang the clouds on invisible thread from the shelf above.

Laura flips onto her back to stare up at the house and its sky. "Doesn't look like a cloud. Looks more like a fluffy bomb."

"There is no such thing as a *fluffy* bomb."

"Or a furry hippopotamus. Without ears. Or a nose." She grins and well, that's okay, cos now I know it's a cloud. Exactly the sort of cloud I want it to be.

"Want to do the next one?" And she nods.

"I don't want to be a man anymore," she says.

"Good."

"Or a saint. Alo says they smell."

Better n better. "Nun?"

"Yup. Only a really, really holy one. I *think* I might be Pope."

"You'd make a great Pope. Scary, but great."

"You'll have to go to Mass when you're the Pope's sister," says Laura. "I'll make you a nun. Sister Squirrel."

"Don't call me squirrel."

"But it's cute."

"I am NOT cute. And nobody calls me squirrel anymore."

"Squirrel. Squirrel Squirrel SQUIRREL," she shouts, running as fast as her veil will carry her. I'm going to regret being nice to her before the day is out.

Acknowledgements

To my beta readers and all the friends and readers who encouraged me to take the dive and publish, who have read and loved my work....THANK YOU! Especially to Patricia Groves, Caroline Farrell, Jean O'Sullivan, Ellie Lundy, Rose Mullin, Emer Lorenz, Lucille Redmond, Claire Hennessy and Patrick Chapman. To Javaholics cafe in Fairview where, even if they didn't know it, lots of this book was rewritten!

And, for believing in me and living with someone who carries many worlds in her head, Libby Sedgwick and Leo Lundy.

To Aoife Henkes, sublime graphic artist and wonderfully talented person, for the cover.

To Barbara Henkes for the photo of me.

To Maynooth University and Kildare County Council Library & Arts Services whose Residency in this academic year (2016-7) has allowed me the time and focus to get this book out there.

L. J. SEDGWICK is addicted to words.  It's the way things are. Despite learning it wasn't a good thing to use five syllable words in the playground of her junior school, her love affair with words continued until, finally, she could launch herself on the unsuspecting world as a journalist and playwright, as well as the worst waitress ever, dog walker, dressing as a Christmas tree to sell milk – and now, finally, novelist.

Along the way, she became an award-winning screenwriter whose work spans genres and form. She has written feature films, television drama and children's series, short films, radio plays and game narrative. Her award-winning series, *Punky* has been recognised as the first mainstream cartoon series in the world in which the main character has special needs and is currently available in over 100 countries. She is currently Screenwriter-in-Residence at Maynooth University and Kildare Co. Council Library & Arts Service.

In addition to screenwriting credits, Lindsay is a prolific playwright whose work has been produced throughout Ireland and in the UK and whose writing has been described as 'gripping,' 'gut-wrenching' and 'seductive'.

For more information on Dad's Red Dress or to read more by this author:

www.lindsayjsedgwick.com
Twitter: @DadsRedDress
Facebook: www.facebook.com/DadsRedDress/

73865654R00163

Made in the USA
Columbia, SC
19 July 2017